A Closet Full of Masks

Susan Snowden

For Nancy,
I hope you enjoy
these Southern Stories!
A number of them are
set in Atlanta.
Best,
Susan

Also by Susan Snowden

Southern Fried Lies

A novel

A Closet Full of Masks

A novella and stories by

Susan Snowden

Archer Hill

Archer Hill Publishing
Columbia, South Carolina

This is a work of fiction. Names, characters, places, and incidents are either the product of the author's imagination or are used fictitiously.

Cover and text design by Tomas Grignon

Cover photograph by Selimaksan/iStock

Archer Hill Publishing
P.O. Box 23341
Columbia, SC 29224-3341
www.archerhillpublishing.com

Printed in the United States of America

ISBN 978-0-9853301-7-0
Library of Congress Control Number: 2015911629

For Aedan, Silas, and Jacob Palmer

Contents

Novella

Stories

There are quantities of human beings,
but there are many more faces,
for each person has several.

RAINER MARIA RILKE

A Closet Full of Masks

A novella

I.

I HAVE NO IDEA how I got into one of the best art schools in the South, maybe the country, but I do know this: my mother, Catherine Atwater Claiborne, was behind it. I picture her as the Wizardess of Oz, grinning behind a blood-red velvet curtain, pulling strings or pushing buttons—whatever wizards and wizardesses do to control things in their world. In the Land of Catherine that year, the work at hand was getting me into art school so I could become the Great American Artist.

My older brother, Ben, had decided to be an architect, quashing Mother's dream that he become the Great American Novelist. After a nervous breakdown over that, she focused on me. I'd shown a teensy glimmer of talent for drawing, which the wizardess believed, if nurtured, could launch me to fame and fortune. Sad to say, due to more interest in socializing than studying I made rotten grades during my senior year. But she plucked her magic strings and got me into an excellent college in Florida. I wasn't thrilled but couldn't think of an excuse not to go. Besides, bucking Catherine would cause my family a mountain of misery.

So to begin at the beginning, it was August 1964 when I arrived at the "renowned" (Mother's word) Flagler College of Art and Design. Located in south Florida, it's not pleasant in summer, unless you enjoy frying your feet like bacon through the soles of your shoes. I grew up in Atlanta; I understand heat and humidity, but temperatures down there blew tops off thermometers. The cute, crisp tops Mother insisted I take were limp and pitiful by ten in the morning.

Freshmen checked in for orientation a week before classes started. We toured the campus, attended assemblies, met faculty members at receptions. Trekking through an on-campus gallery that showcased students' work, I grabbed my roommate's arm. "I'm in big trouble, Gina," I whispered. "My stuff looks like kindergarten compared to this."

Gina shook her head. "I'm pretty much screwed," she said, huffing. Gina was plump, and we'd trudged around in ninety degree heat all morning.

"You're not screwed," I said. "You're every bit as good as these people." I'd seen her portfolio. Her paintings were amazing—intricate tapestry-like oils and acrylics.

She fanned herself with the gallery guide, a glazed look in her eyes.

In a school where 90 percent of the students were Floridians, Gina Moore and I stood out like warts on a witch's nose, she being from Roanoke, Virginia, and me from Atlanta. We didn't dress or act like the other girls, rich snobs who'd studied art since they were little—in private classes, with tutors, during summers abroad at swoopy art camps. Gina said she took art in high school, but for only a year. I'd had a drawing class two months before at the Atlanta Art Institute.

"I can't believe these bitches," Gina grumbled on our second night, her frosted brown hair flying in the wind from the box fan she'd bought to augment the a.c. in our room. "They look like starving sea birds in their tattered cut-offs and t-shirts."

I agreed. Gina and I were more like tropical birds escaped from pet store cages, she in color-blocked muumuus and me in pastel shorts and flowered tops. I detested the clothes I'd brought but Mother said they were "au courant," that all the girls would be wearing similar outfits. I should have challenged her on that. How would she know? She hadn't been to Florida in years.

As for the male students, they looked like Atlanta's homeless men in their dingy stretched-out shirts and holey jeans. Everybody wore cheap rubber flip-flops. Fine by me; I'd been wearing them all summer. But when you walked down a hall your ears were bombarded by flip-flops slapping the bottoms of feet.

On our fourth night Gina started packing. She planned to depart on Saturday morning at sunup—no signing out, nothing. We hadn't started classes officially, so the college column in her education record would stay blank.

As I sipped iced tea and watched her load sheets and towels into a cardboard box, I asked if she could drop me off in Atlanta.

"Smart girl," she said. "You figured it out."

I shrugged. "They'd send me home in a week or two anyway. Why not cut bait now."

Our reasons for leaving were different. Gina would have done well; she was as talented as anyone there, but she missed her boyfriend, Mike. They'd known each other since first grade.

"What're you gonna do?" I asked her.

"I have no idea."

"What'll your parents say?"

"I'm the baby; I can do no wrong."

Well, I'm not the baby in my family and my mother was going to flip, probably end up back in the loony bin.

I liked Gina during our week as roommates but loved her after the long drive to Atlanta. She cursed like a pool hall guy and smoked Pall Malls. She wore no makeup and she'd arrived at snooty Flagler with paint under her fingernails. That's what I called cool. Her dad was head of a hospital and she had good table manners, which in Mother's book is a sure sign of "good breeding," but Gina was no Southern belle. She wasn't the least bit interested in Emily Post etiquette, and she said exactly what she thought. Card-carrying belles say only what people want to hear.

Halfway through our twelve-hour trip I decided to be like Gina, pull off my happy-go-lucky mask and recap my high school years for her. By the time we reached Valdosta, I had told her about being locked in the tower by the queen (Mother), about the queen's various breakdowns, and my quest to convince the king (Daddy) she needed help.

She didn't seem shocked. "How does it feel being out of the tower?"

"It's only been a few days," I said. And then it hit me: I was headed right back to the castle keep. Had I lost my mind?

When we got to my house it was close to midnight. I had only one suitcase; my footlocker and box of bedding wouldn't fit in Gina's Corvair, so I'd left them in our room. "Thanks," I said and hugged her. "Call me. Let me know what happens."

She said she would but I think we both knew she wouldn't. I imagined she would get a job and marry Mike in the near future. I didn't know what to do next. For now I was steeling myself to face Mother.

"Good luck," Gina said and pulled off.

I'd given her only the Cliff Notes version of life with Catherine, so she didn't know I needed more than luck. At thirteen life as I'd known it ended. My brother Ben dropped out of Vanderbilt, which he didn't like, and he was sick of Mother calling him day and night. He announced his decision at Christmas. Mother went berserk. They had a huge fight and he left the next day, got on a bus to New Orleans. He got a job, found an apartment, and cut Mother off—wouldn't call her, write, or visit. That went on until my senior year when he came home for my graduation.

In the interim Mother clamped down on me, told me what to wear, black-balled my friends, grounded me for the slightest infraction—like getting home ten minutes past my curfew. I was a jailbird, really, with limited yard privileges. After what happened with Ben, I'm sure she was afraid of losing me too; I see that now. Back then I just wanted to escape, or somehow "fix" her so she'd be like the normal mothers in our neighborhood. For several years all she did was slam doors, sit in her room and cry, or guzzle scotch on the rocks. Then suddenly she launched her mission to get me into art school. At first she targeted the Ringling School in Sarasota, but her friend Amelia said Flagler was more prestigious; that's all it took for her to switch gears. When I got an acceptance letter from Flagler, fireworks shot up over the Land of

Catherine. She hadn't been that happy in a long time.

Daddy was in the kitchen. I figured Mother was watching *The Late Show*, that Daddy was hovering nearby to make sure she didn't fall asleep smoking and set our house on fire; she'd done that before.

When I walked in he squinted. "You're home?" he said in a low voice.

I had planned to be rational and calm. Instead, I hung my head and cried.

"What is it, honey?" he said, turning on the hall light and leading me into the living room. We sat in the two chairs flanking the fireplace, and between sniffling and wiping my nose I explained why I was back. Daddy nodded, said, "Your mother . . ." then stopped.

"Daddy, I couldn't bring all my stuff. It wouldn't fit in my friend's car." I told him about Gina, how she'd dropped out too. I also confessed that we left without telling anyone.

"We'll get this ironed out, sweetie. You go on to bed."

Mother surprised me as much as my boo-hooing had the night before. When I finally got up, Chris and Annie, my younger brother and sister, had gone off with friends. My parents were at the breakfast room table. I could tell from Mother's expression that Daddy had told her my story.

"What are your plans?" she asked. No hug; not even hello. But she didn't sound angry.

I rubbed my itchy, dry eyelids.

"Do you want me to see if the Art Institute will take you at this late date? Do you want to get a job?"

I definitely didn't want to go to the Atlanta Art Institute. That would mean living at home. "Uh . . . I'm not sure."

Mother looked at Daddy, who was buttering his toast. She sighed. "Well, we need to get your belongings home. What did your advisor say?"

I lied. "She wasn't in her office."

"You didn't officially withdraw? You just marched out?"

"It was the weekend . . . nobody was around."

She smirked, but didn't charge off to her room and slam the door. It was eerie. She turned to Daddy. "Ed." Now he was forking scrambled eggs into his mouth. "Edward," she repeated, louder. He looked up. "When can you drive down to collect Sarah's things?"

He said he would go the following weekend; he'd take Moses with him to help. Moses was the maintenance man at Daddy's office. He fixed all kinds of things, like leaky faucets and broken light switches.

"Mother, can I go over to Laurie's?"

She shot me her old rattlesnake look. "Hasn't she left for Kirkland?"

Kirkland College. "I don't think so. I think it's next week."

"Well, my dear, you just chug on over. You just have yourself a wonderful time. Whoop-de-doo."

Now *that* was Catherine; that was the mother I knew. I stood up to go to my room.

"I'll have to withdraw you over the phone, I suppose."

I shrugged.

"You know, money doesn't grow on trees, Sarah."

Here we go.

"Are you the least bit concerned that we might not get your tuition back?"

"Yes, ma'am." I lied again. I hadn't thought about that. I just wanted out before they kicked me out. Down there, I felt like a toddler who'd wandered into Rembrandt's studio with crayons and a coloring book.

"You didn't wanna go to that school anyway," Laurie said. "What'd your mom say?"

"She didn't seem that upset. She was worried about the money, but there was no blowup."

"You've gotta be kidding."

Laurie had lived through the war years between Mother and me. She knew all about her ridiculous rules and, of course, the beating when I was fifteen that forced me to run away. "I was expecting her to flip, but . . . nothing. She asked me what my plans are now, almost in a normal voice."

"Well, I know what you're gonna do, Claiborne. You're going to Kirkland with me."

I didn't want to go to an all-girls college in some backwater South Carolina town, but that's where I landed. It was either that or sell girls' frilly frocks at Schuman's Sub-Deb Shop in Buckhead.

Since I seemed frozen about what to do next, the wizardess punched buttons on her control panel and convinced Roz Schuman to give me a job. She said I could work for Roz, live at home, and apply to colleges for the following fall. I think she hoped I would enroll at Georgia State, which is in downtown Atlanta—with no dorms. I would have to live at home in her lovely Georgian-style prison on Westchester Boulevard. She could use me, of course, to drive Chris and

Annie around. Well, I would rather have gotten in the bathtub and plugged in our toaster than work as a shop girl and live with Catherine, so I pulled strings myself and got into Kirkland. Laurie's uncle was on the board of trustees there, which helped.

I wasn't thrilled about heading off to Mayville, South Caro-Nowhere, but I had no other ideas. Counselors at my high school didn't encourage girls to consider college; they counted on us getting married, at least the pretty ones. We would become biscuit-makers. We would cook and wash clothes and iron and pop out babies while our husbands paid the bills; therefore, the counselors helped only boys make college plans.

Laurie gave me her Kirkland brochure to get me fired up about going. The campus did look pretty: towering oak trees, deep green grass, white-columned buildings. "Do you know anyone there?" I asked her. "Or anybody else going from Atlanta?"

"Yeah, Anna Spurling, my cousin. You met her one time. They live in Brookwood Hills."

I didn't remember. "That's it? One person?"

"Relax. Anna can introduce us to everybody. She's a senior."

"It seems weird going to college with no guys around. I mean, the world is coed. Shouldn't college be coed?"

"Yeah, and it'll be coed every weekend. There's a bunch of men's schools in the area."

I sighed.

"Listen, the girls go to classes and study all week, then party like crazy on weekends. And Myrtle Beach isn't that far."

II.

DADDY DELIVERED ME to Kirkland; Mother rarely left the house anymore except to buy groceries or pick up dry-cleaning. Freshmen weren't allowed to have cars on campus, so my old Chevy Bel Air, "Beulah," would stay parked until I went home for Christmas.

During the last hour of the trip, I began to understand the expression "My heart sank." Mine was sinking fast, plummeting, as the landscape got bleaker and bleaker. It was flat, flat land with scrubby pine trees here and there. We passed small farmhouses with sagging front porches and weather-beaten barns. Now and then I'd spot a bony cow or a sway-back horse grazing on brown grass. Within a half hour we must have passed three or four rundown churches with dirt parking lots, one with a wooden cross assuring passersby that Jesus Saves. Another whitewashed cross by a roadside cemetery read "Blood" and "Secured" on the tall post and "Redemption" on the cross post.

"How do you read that, Daddy? Is it 'Blood Redemption Secured' or 'Blood Secured Redemption'?"

"What?"

"That cross we just passed? How are you supposed to read it?"

"Oh, I don't know, sweetie; I didn't notice it."

I like words. I read a lot and look up words I don't know, then try to use them if I can. My English teacher in ninth grade said if you use a word three times it's yours, part of your vocabulary. It was a good thing I'd packed my dictionary because I wasn't sure what "redemption" meant. I liked the sound of it.

When we finally reached Mayville my jaw dropped. The "downtown" was only a handful of blocks with tiny storefronts. There were three traffic lights, one broken and blinking. I felt sick.

"Let's find a place to eat," Daddy said. "We can't check you in until two."

"We passed a Dairy Queen when we turned off the highway."

"Oh, there'll be restaurants here on the main drag," he said. He turned the radio down; I'd had rock 'n' roll blaring for an hour but it was now mostly static—more proof we were in the middle of nowhere.

We crawled down Main Street and spotted a little café: Billy's Kitchen. It had dirty windows, one with "Home Cookin'" painted on it in squiggly letters. I groaned.

Daddy chuckled. "You'd be surprised at how good the food is in these places. I've been in towns like this all over the Carolinas."

"Really?" I said. "What for?"

"Designing substations for the local power companies."

I'd seen big buildings my father's company designed in Atlanta. I couldn't imagine this one-horse town having anything like that. I also didn't know what a substation was; another word to look up.

Billy, or whoever the chef was in that place, was OK in my opinion. The food was actually good—lots of fresh vegetables (not cooked to mush!), homemade biscuits, a choice of fried chicken or baked ham. I felt better after I'd eaten and ordered a second Coke to go. In the South Coca-Cola takes care of all ailments: settles your stomach, perks you up if you're dragging, but—strangely enough—calms your nerves when you're upset.

At the end of Main Street a sign pointed to the college. I was anxious to get there but Daddy said we still had time to kill. "Let's walk," he said. "Pack down that big lunch."

"OK, but we can stroll through this whole town in five minutes." I couldn't imagine what kids did for fun here.

I wasn't far off in my time estimate. It took us all of twenty minutes to tour "bustling" Main Street. "Can we go now, Daddy?" I said. "I, uh, need a restroom."

"I don't see why not." He looked at his watch. "They won't care if we're a few minutes early."

The college had set up a reception area in the dining hall with punch and cookies, and coffee for the parents. Girls who looked much younger than me were sniffling and hugging their mothers good-bye. We spotted Laurie and her mom—her father was away on business, as always—and we walked over to speak to them. Daddy chatted with Mrs. Riley while Laurie and I went to get some punch. Her cousin Anna and another older girl, dressed like they were going to church, were serving.

"What's with the white gloves?" Laurie teased Anna.

"You just wait, cuz. It pays to get on their good side." She nodded toward a clutch of straight-laced old ladies shaking hands with parents.

Laurie reminded Anna who I was.

"Glad Laurie talked you into coming," she said. "Whaddaya think?"

"Well, ah, I'm not sure about Mayville; I might go nuts here."

"Oh, we usually clear out on weekends."

The other girl serving punch cackled. "Road trip, road trip."

"Road trip, road trip," Anna chanted.

They "warr-harred" and slapped hands. Anna leaned over and whispered, "We'll show you the ropes, Sarah. Nobody worries about the rules around here."

Daddy and Mrs. Riley came over to report that we didn't have to haul our bags to our rooms; some local high school boys had been recruited to work as porters. Mrs. Riley wanted to see Laurie's room, so off they went. Daddy said it was a long trip back to Atlanta and that he'd take off unless I wanted him to go with me. I didn't really, since mostly mothers would be checking out their daughters' rooms. With a lump in my throat I hugged him, thanked him for driving me over, then set out to find my room. Unfortunately, Laurie and I couldn't be together since her roommate had been assigned months before.

Thayer Hall was three stories and I found my room on the top floor, where most of the freshmen were assigned to suites consisting of two rooms—two girls in each room—connected by a bathroom. I knocked twice, cracked the door, and peered in. Stretched out on one of the twin beds was a giant girl with a very small head. "Are you Sarah?" she asked in a high voice that didn't match her body. "I'm Duke."

"Oh . . . I, um . . . I must be in the wrong place. I'm s'posed to be rooming with"—I looked down at my assignment sheet—"Jane Inman."

"That's me," she squeaked, "but everybody calls me Duke." She stood up and stretched. She had to be over six feet tall. "I'm from Daytona Beach. You've heard of the Daytona 500, right? My brother works in the pits. He can get us in anytime we want. I got to help him change a tire at the last race. You want to come home with me at Christmas? There won't be any races, but we can . . ." On and on she chattered.

The inside of my head felt like a shaken-up snow globe. Sitting in my dorm room at Kirkland College on the edge of Tiny Town, South Carolina, just two weeks after sitting in my ritzy room in Florida, was too much to process. Instead of a palm tree, a giant hemlock swayed in the breeze outside my window. And instead of sharing space with cool Gina Moore from Roanoke, I got Big Duke from Daytona. For the life of me, I couldn't imagine why they'd matched me up with Jane Inman. We had exactly two things in common. We were both tall and we were both Episcopalians. That was it. Hardly seemed grounds for two people to live happily in a tiny room together for a year.

As it turned out, "Duke" wasn't nearly as talkative as she'd been when we first met; she must have been nervous that day. She was a sweet person, really, but my high school friends would have referred to her as "poor thing." She spent her free time popping popcorn illegally in her closet and selling it to anyone on our hall who was interested. I told her that "Jane" was a nice name, that she should drop the old nickname and make a new start, but she said she liked it. Where that name came from she didn't say, but she did resemble John "Duke" Wayne, the cowboy movie star. She had about two inches of hair on her arms too.

Laurie was in a dorm across campus and hadn't fared well in the roommate department either. She'd been paired with another "poor thing": Martha Stubbs, a homely girl with frizzy mouse-brown hair and eyes that pointed in different directions. I first met Martha in Laurie's room; later she was assigned as my lab partner in biology. Once when we were dissecting a fetal pig, one of her eyes watched me probe its tiny aorta while the other one spun around the room. Very disconcerting.

Right away, Anna Spurling introduced us to the cool girls who hung out in the canteen, a big room with a snack bar, tables and chairs, and a juke box. That first night, some of the girls were dancing to "Sixty-Minute Man"—beach music, Anna said. They were doing the

Shag, a sort of easy-going version of the jitterbug I'd never seen.

After meeting Duke and Martha I had worried that Kirkland was a college for freaks, but the girls in the canteen were beautiful. Every single one must have been homecoming queen at her high school. I didn't fit into the freak or beauty queen category since I'm pretty average. Okay hair. Okay figure. Okay face. About the only thing I get complimented on is my skin. Mother says I have a "peaches and cream" complexion. I had boyfriends in high school, but hordes of guys didn't hover around me, as I'm sure they did these girls.

One of the beauties, a perky brunette with sparkly brown eyes, came over and introduced herself as Cindy Sessions. She handed me a pen and one of those "Hello, My Name Is" tags. "You're a freshman, right?" Before I could answer she said, "You'd best be nice to me. Rat Week starts Monday and I'm in charge."

"Rat Week?"

She grinned. "You'll find out."

Laurie and I went out the back door of the canteen and sat on the steps. We were close to a smelly trashcan, so we moved out to a wrought iron bench under the trees. Laurie was in a snit; she'd found out that freshmen couldn't have phones in their rooms. "There's one goddamn pay phone on my hall," she said. "How's Roy gonna call?"

"I guess he'll call and whoever answers will go get you."

"Doubt it. That phone'll be tied up every night."

Laurie had gone steady with Roy since ninth grade. They were inseparable and I'd known she would miss him. He was back in Atlanta, a sophomore at Georgia Tech.

"If only I could've gone to Georgia State," Laurie said.

"Yeah, but you would've had to live at home."

"That wasn't the problem. My father's a miser, as I've told you, and

Uncle Whit got me in here for practically nothing."

Suddenly a bell like a fire alarm rang. "That means dinner," I said. "I'm starved."

Laurie stuck her finger in her mouth and leaned over like she was going to barf. "I'm not going," she said and stood up. "I'm sick at my stomach."

The next day I met my suite mate, Barbara Page from Pageland, South Carolina. She was thin and pretty with auburn hair and huge green eyes she played up with fifty pounds of mascara. Turned out the town wasn't named for her family, but for some rich guy from England named Page. The Pages Barbara belonged to must have been poor because she bragged about her jewelry. Mother says people who don't have much are the ones who talk about their stuff all the time.

"My great aunt gave me this one," Barbara said, sticking an emerald and gold ring up to my eyes. "And these." She picked up three gold bracelets.

"I don't have any decent jewelry," I said. I pointed at the ruby ring on my little finger. "Just this."

"You got any costume jewelry?"

"A few bangle bracelets."

"Bring 'em in here," she said.

I fetched them like a good dog and she showed me how to lacquer them with clear fingernail polish to make them shine.

"How'd you swing getting this room by yourself?" I asked.

"My roommate changed her mind about coming at the last minute."

"Well, if you get lonesome I'll swap with you. Duke's real easy-going, and think of all that free popcorn."

She rolled her eyes. "Thanks. 'Preciate the offer."

Freshmen were required to take English, math, history, a science, and a language. I begged my advisor to get me out of math, and when she saw my grades from high school she thought it was a good idea. "You're a bit lopsided academically, Miss Claiborne." She smiled, looking down at my records. "Top two percentile in verbal skills on the SATs; bottom two in math."

Yeah, well. What could I say?

She put me down for sociology, which sounded interesting, and I picked Spanish for my language. I'd taken two years of it in high school.

The only course I had with Laurie was sociology—"sosh," we called it. After our first class we ate in the cafeteria with Anna and her friend Gail, who told us about Rat Week. She said the junior and senior girls would order freshmen around, give us chores like ironing their clothes and cleaning their toilets. The week would culminate in a skit night. We would form teams and plan skits; whoever staged the best one would be rewarded.

That night we rats were given yellow bows to wear in our hair to mark us as freshmen. Duke said she wasn't wearing any bow. "You've got to, Jane," I said. Sometimes I couldn't bring myself to call her Duke. "Just go along with them and this'll be a breeze."

How naïve of me.

III.

KIRKLAND BILLED ITSELF as a nondenominational liberal arts college, but according to the history section in the catalog it had Methodist roots. Knowing that, I later wondered why they would allow a practice as cruel as Rat Week. Wouldn't some Christian values have filtered down? Freshmen were attending classes and studying; we were also trying to keep our clothes and rooms clean, yet just crossing campus took forever. Whenever I saw a junior or senior, I had to stop and drop to my knees in front of her. If I didn't she could make me do a nasty chore. But that inconvenience was nothing. At midnight on the second day of Rat Week two girls in black robes and masks stormed into our room. Duke was studying and I was half-asleep.

"Get up," one ordered Duke in a deep voice. She was armed with a long black umbrella and jabbed it into Duke's stomach. "Open your closet," the other girl said. Duke always locked her closet to protect her popcorn-making paraphernalia, so she fished the key out of her purse and handed it to the girl. I'd gotten out of bed and Deep Voice shoved me. "Open your wardrobe," she barked. I did as I was told. "Get in there, bitch!"

I froze. I'm terrified of being trapped in small spaces.

"Get 'er in there," she directed her sidekick, who barreled into me and had me locked in that dark, stuffy box in no time. My knees weak, I hunkered down on some dirty clothes I'd piled on the floor. After I heard them slam Duke into her closet, I screamed so hard I passed out.

The next day I ate lunch with Duke in the canteen. She usually ate alone and when I saw her sitting by herself I joined her; it was the least I could do since she'd saved my life. She'd managed to spring me just minutes after I lost consciousness.

Barbara Page came in and walked over to our table. She said the dorm mother wanted to see us right away. "What the heck was going on in y'all's room last night?"

"Tell ya later," I said. "Where are we supposed to go?"

"Her apartment."

"Where's that?"

"On the first floor," Duke broke in. "I know where it is."

I hadn't seen Miss Willis but once at the welcome reception. Anna said she was a monster. The older girls called her the Red-Headed Whore. She had orangey-red hair, dyed for sure, but she dressed like my grandmother and wore horn-rimmed glasses; the nickname didn't fit.

"Sit down, ladies," she said, nodding at two faded beige armchairs. "Now, tell me what happened last night."

"I had to do it," Duke said. "I had to help Sarah."

Miss Willis looked at me. Knowing I'd regret it, I told her what happened.

"Can you identify the two students?"

'No, ma'am. They were wearing masks."

"Well, someone has to pay for the damage." She turned to Duke.

"I . . . I don't know who they were," Duke said.

Duke had told me at lunch that she escaped her closet soon after the girls left. She crashed her shoulder into the door a few times and it opened. The door was OK, but the frame had splintered. Next she ripped the handle off my wardrobe, lock and all. That would need to be replaced too.

"I'm sorry about all this, Miss Willis," I said. "I have claustrophobia. I fainted. I guess Duke . . . uh, Jane . . . thought I'd suffocated in there."

Duke nodded. "I thought she was dead."

As a dorm mother at Kirkland for years, Miss Willis must have honed her sleuthing skills because she routed out the criminals fast. By the end of the day both girls were on restriction; they couldn't leave campus for a month. Their parents had been contacted and would share the cost of mopping up their daughters' mess.

Laurie was worried about me. Apparently, the stool pigeon who squealed on the two girls was already regretting it. "I don't know the details," she said. "Just be careful."

In the middle of the night two different masked girls came for us, one as wide as Duke but shorter, and one about my size—thin, maybe five seven or eight. We should've both been asleep, but Duke was ironing. They instructed us to put raincoats on over our pajamas (nightgown in my case) because we were crossing the quadrangle to their dorm. Duke shook her head no, planted her feet behind the ironing board, and held up the iron—hot side pointed toward them. Each time the chunky girl approached her, Duke pushed the button and blasted scalding steam at her. The scene would have been funny under different circumstances, Duke standing stone-faced, firing at the enemy. Big Duke was going nowhere.

I, on the other hand, was blindfolded and marched downstairs, across pavement and grass, through doors, up two flights of stairs.

When we reached our destination they took off the blindfold. We were in a large room lit only by candles. Three more masked girls were seated at a table, a bottle of vodka in the middle. My "guards" sat me down in a straight-back chair a few feet in front of them.

"Miss Claiborne, you were foolish. You'll have to pay," the middle girl at the table said. She had a thick Southern accent. Right away I recognized the voice, *and* the brown curl poking out of her stocking cap. Cindy Sessions. Lovely former Cotton Queen from Gaffney, South Carolina, adored by every authority figure at Kirkland. For some reason I wasn't scared. Stupid of me, since they could easily lock me in a closet again.

Cindy continued. "If you'd sat quietly in your wardrobe, you would have been freed within the hour."

Fat lot this bimbo knows about phobias, I thought. My heart fluttered a little, but stopped when I remembered to breathe.

"You have nothing to say for yourself?" Cindy chided.

"I have claustrophobia."

Someone behind me said, "Awww, bless your heart."

Cindy Sessions leaned over and whispered to the girl on her right; the girl got up and left the room. We sat in silence for a few minutes and then I heard footsteps. I turned my head enough to see girls in dark clothes filing in and sitting on the floor against the back wall.

Cindy cleared her throat. "OK, let's begin," she said. "We're gathered tonight to hear a story. Miss Claiborne here is going to treat us to a story."

"But I don't—"

"Shut up!" she shrieked, slamming her fist on the table. "Now, tell us about the first time you got fucked."

Oh, lord.

"We'd like details, please, not an overview."

The girls in back laughed.

I thought of how I'd stood up to Mother so many times when she was grilling me. "Please forgive me, ma'am," I said in a syrupy voice, "but I haven't had that experience."

Lots of snickers from the peanut gallery.

"Pour her a drink, Number One," Cindy said, nodding to my left. With that, the big girl who'd been intimidated by Duke's iron stepped up to the table. She filled the glass with vodka, then handed it to me.

"Drink up," Cindy said. "It'll jog your memory." I took a few swallows hoping it would calm my nerves. "The whole thing. Empty it."

"No thank you," I purred.

Cindy stood. "Listen, scum. Cut the sarcasm!" This time she slapped the table with her open palm.

I just smiled and batted my eyelashes.

"Have it your way," she said. "Number Two? You know what to do."

The girl on my right duct-taped my arms behind the chair, yanked my head back by my hair. Then Number One poured vodka down my throat. I coughed and gagged, then pitched forward, landing on my knees and forehead, the chair still attached to me. It took both girls to return me, and the chair, to an upright position.

"Well, pond scum, shall we try again?" Cindy said. "How big was his dick? Your first love's, that is."

More twittering and giggles from the audience.

My kneecaps were throbbing, so I decided to give them what they wanted. That or maybe die here. "All right, I'll answer your questions," I said, then responded to each one in a matter-of-fact tone. I made up every word because the truth was I hadn't gone all the way. Over the summer my boyfriend Alan and I almost did, but I stopped him. He was going off to Stanford and I knew he'd forget me, which happens to girls in movies a lot.

That wasn't the only reason I held out, though. Mother accused me of being a slut when I was fourteen, and I wanted to prove her wrong. So while some of my friends were having sex to rebel against their strict parents, I was rebelling against my mother by *not* doing it. Luckily, I'd heard enough and read enough to fool Cindy Sessions. Plus, I'd learned to lie by example; Mother is World Champion of Liars. Of course, she lies to save face among her friends. I lied that night to keep from choking to death.

"You're the talk of the town," Laurie said. "What the hell did you tell them?"

"You don't want to know."

"Anna said you had everybody rolling on the floor."

"Anna was there?"

"Yeah. She said they knew you were making it all up, but it was so funny they didn't care."

"Cindy Sessions was the ring leader. I recognized her."

"She's such a phony. Anna says she brown-noses all the professors, but she's the wildest girl on campus."

"Well, I told 'em this guy pinched my boobs real hard and it hurt, but then he kissed and licked my whole body, which felt really great and got me in the mood. Cindy kept interrupting, demanding details."

"Like?"

"Oh, you know. Like how hairy was he and how long was his ding-dong."

"Gross."

"I said, 'Oh, gosh, it wasn't very long, you know . . . but it was *really* wide. Kinda like a Campbell's soup can.' They liked that."

"Jesus, Claiborne!"

In the midst of the pranks and punishments, we rats were supposed to be planning our skits. I'd had only four hours of sleep but dragged myself over to my team's first meeting. It was Barbara Page, me, and the four girls from the suite next door. Duke refused to take part in skit night, and I wondered what consequences she might face. She wouldn't scare Cindy Sessions with a steam iron.

Missy Pollard, a girl from a mill town south of Mayville, convinced everyone but me that we should black our faces, line up on stage, and do "nigger cheers." Her exact words. I couldn't believe it. I thought it was a sick idea, but didn't say so. Instead, I suggested something different. "Why don't we dress up like regular cheerleaders? We can write a cheer about Kirkland, maybe something about the smart, beautiful seniors."

"Boring," said Missy, faking a yawn.

"What should we wear?" Barbara asked.

Judy Cox wondered how we could black our faces.

I was ignored; the decision was made.

I went to sociology in spite of the purple and yellow bruise on my forehead. Barbara covered it for me with heavy pancake makeup. She was an expert in makeup, not just jewelry. Laurie didn't show up and I wondered if she too had been tortured for some rat infraction. After class I grabbed an egg salad sandwich in plastic wrap at the canteen and went to check on her. She was in bed with a stomach bug, her face gray.

"Did you go to the infirmary?"

"Nah. Martha brought me a Coke and some aspirin."

"Has Roy called?"

"Last night. I think that's why I'm sick."

"Y'all had a fight?"

"No, but he can't come this weekend. He *says* he's gotta cram for a calculus quiz."

"You don't believe him?"

"He sounded strange. Maybe he's met somebody."

"Roy's not like that."

She sighed. "I just wish I was there . . . in Atlanta."

I reminded her of their grand plan. She'd do two years at Kirkland while he worked hard at Tech and graduated. Then they'd find jobs and get married.

She started to cry. "I know . . . I know, I know. I just don't think I can wait."

That night, on top of reading a chapter for history and reviewing Spanish vocabulary, I had to memorize the awful cheers. I dreaded Friday night.

Barbara and I practiced on Thursday, then met with the others for a run-through. Missy Pollard showed us black grease paint she'd "borrowed" from the drama club's closet, and handed out bandanas. "Since we don't have kinky hair we'll wear these," she said, giggling. She tied one on her head like Aunt Jemima on the pancake box.

Everyone was charged up about winning the competition. They

carried on like they were auditioning for the Rockettes. Missy lined us up and watched us shout out the cheers in sync with the moves and waving our pom-poms. The first cheer went:

You kin squeeze de limon to git de juice
But to beat Booker T just ain't no use.
Ray, Booker! Rah, T
Rah, ray, Booker T
Fight, Tigers, fight!
Up my leg and down my spine
Booker T, Booker T, hold dat line!

"Stop, stop!" Missy hollered before we could go on to the next cheer. "Pick up the tempo! Y'all look half-asleep."

This went on for an hour before Missy was satisfied. I, thank heavens, wouldn't be performing. On the final "YAY!" and leap into the air, I came crashing down like a building smacked by a wrecking ball. I twisted my ankle and couldn't get up. Barbara ran to get Duke, who helped me hobble to the infirmary. The show had to go on, of course, but Sarah Claiborne wouldn't be part of Missy's pep squad.

Hallelujah!

Getting injured was lucky for me. I met a cute guy at the hospital—Lewis Jordan. He x-rayed my ankle to see if it was broken, which entailed him moving my foot three or four times. After I groaned and grumbled about him torturing me, he asked me out. He seemed nice enough. He was polite and had one of those wide open faces that look honest, so I accepted. The idea of escaping Kirkland relieved the pain in my ankle right away, although it might've been the Darvon they gave me. Due to Lewis's schedule we couldn't go till the following Friday. Eight days to wait.

The school nurse was waiting in the lobby when I clunked out on crutches, my ankle wrapped in an Ace bandage. The ER doctor came out with me, told her it was sprained. He said I should ice it and keep it elevated for a few days.

Things were definitely looking up. I got out of doing the racist cheers but was allowed to watch the skits, my ankle propped up on a chair in the aisle. My "team" took first place, which said more about the other performances than theirs. It was hard not to laugh as I listened to off-key hymns, an accordionist playing a polka with girls twirling behind her, and four eggheads reciting the prologue to *The Canterbury Tales*. Middle English spoken with Southern accents is hilarious.

Laurie's team came in second. Laurie lip-synched "Heat Wave" by Martha and the Vandellas as her teammates danced and doo-wopped. A girl from Charlotte lounged on a baby grand singing "You and the Night and the Music" in a tight red dress. She'd been odd man out when we formed teams, so she was forced to do a solo; Cindy let a junior accompany her. She deserved first prize, but she came in third.

All of the winners were treated to a party in the canteen on Saturday. Again, the seniors let me come. The food was great—hamburgers and hotdogs grilled outside by a guy who worked in the cafeteria; potato chips, Frito's, peanuts and pretzels; Jell-O salad and two layer cakes.

The older girls, including Cindy Sessions, treated us like royalty. This new sweet-as-sugar Cindy complimented everyone on their skits and offered to spike their Cokes with bourbon if they were interested. Quite a few were, but I didn't dare. I couldn't risk getting tipsy and falling again. Now and then Cindy slipped behind the jukebox with someone's paper cup, an angelic look on her face. Whenever she passed me, she asked if I'd like some Campbell's soup.

IV.

THE NEXT DAY I stayed in bed with the Ace bandage off, my foot on a pile of pillows. Duke brought me a sandwich and iced tea for lunch; I'd slept through breakfast. While she read one of her *Motor Trend* magazines, I lay there wondering what was going on back home. It was weird that Mother hadn't called. When Ben went off to Vanderbilt she called him daily. I guessed she was punishing me for going off to a school her friends had never heard of. Anyway, if she called now, I would have to lie. I couldn't tell her I was bored in my classes, I'd made no friends, and Laurie was avoiding me. At the party for the skit winners, Laurie never once asked about my upcoming date, and she left after fifteen minutes to call Roy.

Around three o'clock Laurie's roommate, Martha, came by to loan Duke her history notes. I asked her what Laurie was up to.

"She's got an upset stomach."

"Again?"

"She was up all night. She can't keep anything down."

With that I got up, put a raincoat on over my nightgown, and peg-legged over to see her. I'd discovered I could get around better with one crutch than two.

Laurie looked awful. She was lying down, her eyes closed. "Want me to get something for you from the nurse?"

"No . . . but thanks." She opened her eyes and turned her head on the pillow to look at me. "I haven't had my period, Claiborne. I should've started two weeks ago."

"Are you serious? You think you're pregnant?"

"Great news, huh?"

"Did you tell Roy?"

"It's my fault." She shook her head. "I screwed up on my pills. I was trying to pack to come over here, and finish that Kelly Girl job, and see Roy as much as I could, and I—"

"Hold on, hold on," I said, sitting down beside her. She was crying. "Maybe you're just late. It could be nerves . . . from Rat Week and all."

She sniffed and wiped her face. "Don't worry about it," she mumbled, then turned over, her back to me.

"Please call Roy, Laurie. I know y'all can figure this out."

My last thought before falling asleep was that Laurie would be going home. Once she started showing they would kick her out. I dreamed I was sailing a tiny boat out of a cove. When I got to the mouth of the cove and saw the ocean I panicked. There was no way I could sail into those choppy waters alone. That was it. The whole dream. Did it mean I was scared to stay at Kirkland without Laurie? Probably not. Back in March I was in a boat with her and she was nothing but trouble.

My father had a sailboat on Lake Lanier, north of Atlanta. Last spring Laurie and I skipped school one day. We brought bathing suits and beach towels from home and stopped at the Tri-Me Deli for sandwiches. Laurie also bought a six-pack with her fake I.D. Off we went to the lake.

The dockmaster wasn't around that early in the season so we rowed Daddy's dinghy out to his big boat, which was moored in the cove. All day we lazed on the deck sunbathing and yakking. I sipped a beer off and on, then switched to Coke. My stomach swells up if I have more than one beer. Laurie drank the remaining five. I had a terrible time loading her back in the dinghy, rowing back to shore, and getting her to my car.

I stopped worrying about Laurie leaving Kirkland. That day on the lake I'd managed fine by myself.

On Monday I limped off to get breakfast and go to my classes. English was a breeze; we were reading *The Scarlet Letter*, which I'd read at the Howell School in tenth grade. In Spanish class we talked Mr. Monterro into teaching us some cuss words. He was the sweetest man. He'd fled Cuba in a rowboat with his wife and son; they made it to Miami with no shoes, just bathing suits and shirts. At the time he knew only two English words: "cheeseburger" and "shoes."

The poor guy was a lawyer in Havana but had to start over in America. Who knows how he ended up in Mayville, South Carolina, but he was doing a good job teaching us Spanish. We, in turn, were helping him with English. That day we taught him some slang expressions like "cut for the hut," "four on the floor," and "chugalug." Then we asked him the Spanish for "damn" and "hell" and a few other words. He was reluctant, but we hounded him till he agreed. Coming out of class I ran into Barbara Page. She'd borrowed someone's car for the afternoon, a junior she knew from Pageland. "Wanna come?" she asked, jingling keys in front of my face.

"Where to?"

"I don't know. I just need to get out of here. Let's start at the Dairy Queen."

We found the girl's Dodge Dart in student parking. Barbara helped me get in and stuck my crutch in the backseat. The second we pulled out of the front gates we rolled down the windows and turned on the radio—top-volume. As we passed the ancient movie theater on Main Street I pointed. "Look, Barbara, they're showing *Blood Feast*. Sounds quite educational."

"Oh, yeah. We gotta see that one."

On the county road to the Dairy Queen we passed the Blood Redemption Secured cross. I asked Barbara if she was religious.

"Not really," she said. "Everybody in Pageland goes to First Baptist, including my parents. They made me go every Sunday morning . . . and Sunday night . . . and Wednesday night . . . and to choir practice on Thursday."

"Are you serious?"

"Yep. But I quit goin' when I was sixteen."

"Did they give you hell?"

She laughed. "Only every day." She turned the radio down. "Do you know Martha Stubbs?"

"Yeah. She's my friend Laurie's roommate."

"She's in my 'sosh' class; she's always quoting the Bible."

"Laurie says she prays in her closet every night."

"Bless her heart. Maybe she should ask God to fix her googly eyes."

"Barbara!"

We had a blast that afternoon; I thought I might survive Kirkland. Plus, I had Friday night to look forward to. Barbara stopped at the jewelry store on Main Street to drool over a pair of diamond stud earrings. I looked around while she asked the sales clerk about payment plans. Mostly they had watches and wedding rings, but there were six different circle pins in that shop. Girls in Atlanta hadn't worn circle pins in years. Being in Mayville was like visiting a remote outpost on Mars.

Back at school there was a letter in my post box. Pale blue stationery; Mother's handwriting. It took a while but I made it to the pond behind the main building, sat on a bench, and opened it. I was wrong about why she hadn't called. She wasn't punishing me; she was having problems with Annie, my sister. Annie had made friends with a junior who could drive; they'd gone on the expressway to the Varsity one day when they were supposed to be at the library.

My sister was an idiot. She had told Mother all about their adventure! Now she was in deep trouble. I did feel for her, but it was fabulous news for me. The warden would be busy policing her now, not worrying about me.

When Mother mentioned Etha Mae, our maid, I teared up. I missed her. Growing up, I was closer to Mae than Mother. If she knew what was going on over here she'd put me on every prayer chain at her church.

I watched a duck family swim in formation for a while, then went to find Laurie. I'd thought of a solution to her problem. She could go home and marry Roy. He was a good guy; he would do the gentlemanly thing. They could live in an apartment near Tech and she could work while he went to classes. I pictured her lovingly ironing his shirts at night, after she fixed dinner, of course. Right now Laurie couldn't fry an egg, but she could learn. When the baby came her mother could watch it while Laurie was at work. Mrs. Riley didn't do much but play solitaire and watch soap operas all day anyway.

Laurie was waiting for the elevator when I stepped out of it.

"Wanna go to dinner?" I said. "Try some mystery meat?"

"I just had soup at the canteen."

"Oh. Where you headed?"

"To the library." She looked down at my foot. "Can you walk over with me?"

"Sure; just go slow."

"I need to hear about this doctor you're going out with," she said.

"I don't think he's a doctor; he takes x-rays. He's pretty cute."

As we walked I told her my idea.

"I wouldn't leave a baby with Mother!" she said. "She's a drunk, in case you forgot. Anyway, I'm not even sure I'll keep it."

"You might give it away?"

"Don't give me that look. You do stupid things too, you know."

"Like?"

"Like quittin' Flagler after a week."

"I wasn't good enough!" I said, raising my voice. Two girls passing by stared at us. "Let's not talk about art school, OK? This is a lot more serious."

"Gee, really?"

We had stopped at this point, but she wasn't looking at me. I stepped up and stood in front of her. "Does Anna know about this? Have you talked to her?"

"Yes."

"What does she say?"

"Never mind."

She went around me and walked away. I followed. "No discussion, huh?"

Silence.

"Just tell me one thing. Why won't you talk to Roy about this? It takes two to tango, you know . . . as the saying goes. Ha-ha."

She spun around. "Oh for god's sake, Claiborne!"

"I'm serious. I mean, this isn't just *your* problem."

"Shut up!" she said, and a little spit hit my cheek. "Don't talk to me about things you know nothing about."

Oh! I thought. Now I get it. "I see. I haven't screwed anybody so I couldn't possibly understand."

She narrowed her eyes, then took off walking again, me hobbling along on her heels. "Now I know why you've had nothing to do with me since we got here."

"Go get your dinner, Sarah," she snapped over her shoulder and stormed up the library steps.

"Word of advice," I called after her. "If you have to advertise for friends someday, be sure to say 'Virgins need not apply.'"

She jerked the library door open and marched in. I stood there for a minute, my heart pounding. If I could have made it up those steps I would have crashed into that hush-hush library and bellowed "Screw you, Laurie Riley!" Instead I headed across campus as fast as I could, given that my ankle was throbbing. I needed to find Anna Spurling.

Anna had gone into town for dinner, according to her roommate. I waited on a bench across the hall till she got back, which was a good thing; I was able to calm down and sound like a sane person when I told her my plan. "Laurie thought it was a rotten idea," I said. "What should we do?"

"*We* shouldn't do anything. She'll figure this out."

"But—"

"And Laurie's right; your scheme won't work."

"Why? Why not?"

"Think about it. Laurie won't be eighteen till November."

"So?"

"So in Georgia Roy could get arrested, locked up for having sex with a minor."

I had to process that for a minute. "But wouldn't someone have to report him?"

"Right, and my uncle would do it for sure. He can't stand Roy."

I'd only met Laurie's father a few times, so I couldn't argue about that. "Why didn't Laurie just tell me that herself? Why is she stonewalling me?"

"That I can't tell you." She patted my arm. "Let her work this out, Sarah. OK? This is none of our business, really."

I stewed in my room for the next hour. I wanted to ask Laurie why she'd talked me into coming to Kirkland if she planned to ditch me. Then Lewis called and I got my mind off of Laurie. He wanted to make sure our date was still on. I told him it was, that I was living in a zoo and needed to escape.

He laughed. "I feel like that at the hospital."

We talked for a half hour. I found out he was twenty-one, that he'd gone to Clemson for two years but dropped out when his father died; his mom needed help with their farm. For some reason I immediately pictured him feeding chickens. Being from Atlanta I didn't know a thing about farms. Maybe it was a dairy farm. I didn't ask; I didn't want to cross-examine him like Mother would.

"What time are you coming?" I asked him.

"I've got the afternoon off. Would five be too early?"

"No. I'll be ready." I told him to come to the Thayer Hall lobby. "One of the zookeepers will spring me."

Barbara trimmed my hair the next day. I had a layered style called a Bubble, but it had grown out and was limp as a wilted house plant. Barbara cut it so that my natural curl would behave; it looked soft and feathery around my face. "Don't tease it too much," she said.

"You're good. Why didn't you go to beauty school?"

"I wanted to, but my mother wants me to teach school."

"And you had no say in the matter?"

"No. But I'll fix her; I'm gonna flunk out."

"How? Quit going to classes?"

"Nope. I just won't show up for tests."

"Brilliant." I thanked her for the haircut and went back to my room. Martha Stubbs was sitting on my bed bawling, Duke standing beside her. "Something's going on with Laurie," Duke said. "You better go over there."

I could hear a bunch of low voices in Laurie's room, so I knocked and turned the knob. Locked. I knocked harder and the lock clicked. Cindy Sessions opened the door a few inches. "Go back to your room," she said.

"What's going on?"

She shut the door in my face. I thought for a minute, then went down and tapped on the door to Laurie's suite mates' room. No answer. It wasn't locked, so I slipped in and cut through the bathroom to Laurie's room. She was standing against the wall holding her stomach, tears streaming down her face. A big girl—possibly the one who'd poured vodka down my throat—grabbed me, twisted my arm behind my back. I shrieked and she clamped her fat mitt over my mouth. I could do nothing but watch in horror at what was happening.

Cindy Sessions and two of her lackeys stood single-file in front of Laurie. Each of them had a laundry bag stuffed with who knows what. Filthy clothes? Books? One girl would step up, swing the bag like a pendulum, then smash it into Laurie's stomach. With each blow Laurie moaned and doubled over, then struggled to stand up.

The next girl repeated the moves. This time Laurie dropped to her knees and hunched over, her head to the floor. No one said a word but Cindy. "Ginger! Go ahead."

The girl named Ginger was short and muscular. She swung her bag a few times, then slammed it down on Laurie's back.

With that, I bit the big girl's paw; she yelped and let me go. "Stop it!" I screamed. "You're gonna kill her."

Cindy stepped up and slapped me across the face. "Listen, Soup Girl, one word about this and you'll be floatin' on the pond tomorrow. 'Gee, she was homesick,' we'll say, 'but we had no idea it would come to this.'"

Ginger snickered.

"Go away, Sarah," Laurie said in a hoarse voice.

The girl I'd bitten dragged me out to the hall and forced me to the floor. I sat with my back against the wall for a while, my heart racing; when it slowed down I knew one thing for sure: those girls were not beating Laurie against her will.

Back in my room I agonized over what to do. Duke said I should tell Miss Willis and she was right. I hated getting Laurie in trouble, but if they kept beating her she really could die. Duke and I discussed all of this in whispers because Martha was in Duke's closet praying. "She says God talks to her," Duke said. "It's gotta be quiet so she can hear him."

I had prayed hard when my mother was acting crazy and I didn't know what to do. God didn't talk to me, but she did get better. Maybe he answered my prayers, but it took over a year and Laurie needed help now. "I'm going to Miss Willis," I said, rushing out. I was instantly stopped by one of Cindy's bullies, who shoved me back into my room. Cindy was an evil genius; she knew I'd try to report her.

V.

ACCORDING TO MY clock the sun should have come up, but from my bed I could see only thick dark clouds in a low sky, wind whipping the hemlock branches. Duke was asleep, so when her closet door swung open I gasped. Martha stepped out looking dazed, then glided over to the window like a sleepwalker. "The Lord knows what happened," she said, her voice weak. "He's angry." She must have thought God stirred up this tempest in his rage. I didn't say a word, and she left.

I looked out in the hall. Empty, none of Cindy's henchmen around. I needed to shower, get dressed, and . . . I wasn't sure. Check on Laurie? Go straight to Miss Willis? I would have to decide. I didn't want Laurie to get sent home, but she'd been badly beaten and would be scared to ask for help.

When I came out of the bathroom, Duke was awake. Someone was knocking on the door but she hadn't budged. I tightened my robe and cracked the door. It was Anna, smiling sweetly.

"Can I come in?"

I opened the door wide and she stepped in. "Laurie's fine," she said. "She's sleeping."

"She's OK? Do you know what they did to her? You should've seen—"

"I know; I took her to the hospital. We just got back."

"Oh my god!"

"Calm down and I'll tell you what happened," she said. I sat on the end of Duke's bed. "OK, here's what you two need to know. She looked at Duke, then back at me. "Laurie started her period last night. It was very heavy and she was in a lot of pain—terrible cramps—so I took her to the emergency room. She's fine now."

She delivered this message in an everyday voice, the voice people use to say things like "I went shopping today and bought a cute dress."

"That's it? That's the story?"

"That's the story, Sarah." She started out the door, then stopped and turned around. "Don't forget, this is none of our business."

Late that afternoon Laurie showed up at my room acting like nothing had happened, like we'd never had an argument, like I hadn't witnessed her being beaten. Her hair looked dirty and she was pale. I told her to stretch out on Duke's bed. "I can't stay," she said. "Just wondered if I could borrow your 'sosh' notes."

"Sure." I went over to my desk and dug out the notebook. "Hey, you know what? This is the first time you've been to my room."

"Give me a break, Sarah, would ya?"

"I'm sorry. I just . . . I don't know why you . . ." I took a deep breath. "I mean, this whole thing seems so unreal."

"Yeah, but it is real . . . or was."

"Roy's never going to know?"

"Nope."

I rolled my eyes.

"Don't give me that look."

"All right, all right." I got up and started pulling the sheets off my bed.

"When you came back from Florida I thought you were nuts, but I didn't say a word, did I?"

I sighed.

"You haven't drawn a thing since you got here, have you? Did you even bring your sketchbook?"

I spun around. "You sound just like Mother! 'You're wasting your talent, Sarah. You could be a famous artist!' God, Laurie!"

She smirked.

I put my hands on my hips. "Now who's being judgmental? Now who's saying what someone should do with her life?"

She got up and left. I can't say I wasn't upset. Laurie had been my best friend since fifth grade. We went away to camp together; we snuck out to ride our bikes in the middle of the night at thirteen. She listened to me whine—for years—when Mother was being so hard on me.

It took me all of about five, maybe ten, minutes to realize that Laurie was right, really. She'd never told me what I should or shouldn't do; she just listened.

I found her in the cafeteria—alone, thankfully. She didn't acknowledge me when I sat down across from her. "You're right," I said. "I'm a jerk. I'm a know-it-all and an ass and . . . I don't know what else, but I'm sorry."

She put her fork down and sighed.

"If I keep my trap shut for a change, can we start over?"

She hung her head.

"I'm sorry. I'm really, really sorry," I said. "If I—"

"Shut up, Sarah. Please." She looked up. "I feel awful. I feel evil and guilty and—"

"About the baby?"

She sniffed, wiped her eyes with her napkin. "I didn't think it was a baby really, not yet. I don't know why I feel so horrible."

"It probably wasn't a baby yet. You're probably right."

Tears slid down her cheeks. "I had awful dreams after I got back from the hospital . . . about a baby girl."

My stomach knotted like a fist. "I'm so sorry, Laurie."

She blotted her eyes and half-smiled.

Walking back to Thayer Hall I realized my ankle was aching. After five days of step-hopping with one crutch I had decided to limp around with only the Ace bandage for support. Now all I wanted to do was lie down and read—not a textbook. When I left Atlanta for Florida I was halfway through *Intruder in the Dust*. Maybe I could finish it tonight.

Missy Pollard stopped me when I got off the elevator on the third floor. "Your daddy just called," she said. "I was fixin' to stick this on your door." She handed me a scrap of paper.

"Is anything wrong?"

She shrugged. "He just said to call."

I glanced at the note. *Sarah C. call your daddy.*

"At home?"

"Oh . . . sorry. I think he said his office."

I waited for a girl I didn't know to get off the hall phone, my mind racing. If there was a crisis at our house I would have to find some train tracks to take a nap on. Finally I got the phone and dialed Daddy's office; he answered on the first ring, said his secretary had left at five.

"What's wrong, Daddy?"

"Not a thing, sweetie. How are you?"

"I'm fine," I lied. "Everything's fine."

"Good." I could hear him shuffling papers. "I see here you haven't written a check on the account we opened for you."

"I haven't needed to. I think I've still got twenty dollars in my wallet."

He chuckled. "Turned over a new leaf, huh?"

"Ha-ha." I'd been known to go overboard buying records and clothes. "You saw Mayville, Daddy. Where would I spend money?"

"Well, let's see . . ." More papers rattling, a drawer closing.

"I buy snacks at the canteen, but I haven't run out of toothpaste or anything like that."

"Well, just call if you need me to make a deposit."

Daddy is the kindest, hardest-working person on earth. He thinks taking care of his family, money-wise, is his main job. When I was growing up he would never discuss my problems; he just tuned me out. It drove me crazy until I was about sixteen, but I finally got it: he hates thinking about things he can't figure out with his slide rule. I loved him anyway, and these days I appreciated how generous he is. I'd overheard a girl on my hall say she couldn't even afford a candy bar from the vending machine.

"Is everything OK at home?" I asked, holding my breath.

"Yes . . . we're all fine, sweetie."

That's what he would say if my fifteen-year-old sister was drinking white lightning and my little brother was in juvenile detention. He wouldn't want me to worry.

Back in our room, Duke was snoring. She kept weird hours. She napped between classes, slept after dinner, studied and showered in the middle of the night. Maybe she was embarrassed to undress in front of me. Maybe her whole body was as hairy as her arms. Her schedule didn't bother me though; she tiptoed around. Nothing I did disturbed her either. Poor thing slept hard, sawing logs like a lumberjack.

I found *Intruder in the Dust* in the box with my thesaurus and dictionary. Stuck in the front of the book was a long list of words I wanted to look up, words I'd never heard—or seen, even in the SAT study guide. From the first chapter alone I had listed "intractable," "cryptic," "balustrade," "dubiety," "hermetic," and "dross." I started looking up definitions, then realized none of them made sense because I'd forgotten the story. I would have to start over.

After reading the first chapter the word "intractable," meaning "not easily manipulated," made sense. Faulkner must have loved that word; he used it five times in ten pages.

I was looking up "balustrade," which sounded very exotic, when Duke woke up. "Good morning," I sang out. She sat up fast looking panicked. Did she honestly believe it was morning? It was ink black outside. "Only kidding," I said. "Sorry."

She rubbed her eyes. "Are you studying?"

"I'm looking up definitions."

"For English?"

"For me."

"How come?"

I told her I was building my vocabulary, which puzzled her no end. If I said I was emulating my brother Ben, who has a huge vocabulary, she would ask what "emulating" meant. I considered saying I'd rather be called Word Girl than Soup Girl, but I hadn't told her the Campbell's soup saga. Whenever sex came up around Duke, her face flushed and she left the room.

"I just like words," I said, then asked about Martha.

"She didn't show up for English. I guess she's still upset."

"Yeah, well, Laurie's OK now."

"You know that Cindy Sessions girl?"

"What about her?"

"She made Martha scrub the bathroom after Laurie . . ."

She couldn't say the word "miscarried" apparently, or didn't know it. I put down my dictionary. "Martha was over here all night," I said. "Remember? She was praying."

"But Cindy showed up the next morning and made her clean up all the blood."

"Oh no . . . poor Martha."

"She thinks God was punishing her."

"For what? What did she do?"

"Didn't stop those girls."

"Good grief, Duke! I don't know where she goes to church, but I wasn't taught to think of God as this angry, punishing tyrant. Were you?"

Duke frowned. "No."

"I wish there was an Episcopal church here. We could take Martha, try to get her out of believing that."

Duke shrugged. "I don't know why those girls pick on her. I wouldn't do a skit, but they never did anything to me."

Right, I thought. When would *that* shoe drop?

Lewis hadn't told me what we were doing on Friday, so it was hard to decide what to wear. Who knows, maybe his idea of a great date was dining at Dairy Queen, followed by riding his plow around the farm. Mother wouldn't be pleased that I hadn't asked what "attire" our engagement required.

Pedal pushers and Keds were no-no's for Kirkland girls, which left me with two choices: a skirt and blouse or a dress. I pulled out a khaki pleated skirt and yellow oxford cloth blouse, and polished my Weejuns. Wearing pennies in loafers wasn't in around here, so I pried mine out with a nail file. I hoped I could shed my Ace bandage by 5 p.m. Friday.

After classes on Thursday I shampooed and set my hair. It always looks better the day after I wash it, not so fly-away. Barbara Page poked her head in as I was plugging in my dryer. "I'm gettin' beautified for tomorrow night," I said.

"Where'd you get those gigantic rollers?"

"Mr. Paul, the guy who did my hair in Atlanta."

"He sells rollers?"

"Yep. And brushes, hairspray, deep conditioner. He's got a whole corner store in his shop."

Barbara shook her head. "Nothing like that in Pageland. They still do pin curls with bobby pins."

I told her how Mr. Paul makes his "girls" do the shampoos and color and serve you champagne. "He doesn't lift a finger till he cuts and styles you."

"Couldn't he get in trouble for that? I mean, giving alcohol to teenagers?"

"Cops in Atlanta have bigger fish to fry, like people peddling dope and stabbing each other."

She wanted to hear more big city stories, but I needed to get under the dryer; mine sounds like a cement mixer, so she didn't stick around. I sat at my desk and filed my nails thinking about Mr. Paul, how he tried to get his customers drunk.

He had a reputation for being a letch and, sure enough, he tried to kiss me on my sixteenth birthday. I was his last customer and everyone had left. I'd sipped two flutes of champagne under the dryer and could barely walk. He smooshed his fat belly against me and begged for "a little birthday kiss." Most self-respecting Buckhead girls would have pretended it didn't happen, but I laughed in his face, hee-hawed like a donkey. My Southern belle mask must have melted under the dryer.

Mr. Paul got no tip and I never went back. I found a new guy named Mad Dog John, whose shop was in the lobby of the Darlington Apartments. He had tattoos and rode a motorcycle, but he was every bit as good as Mr. Paul.

Coming back from dinner, I answered the pay phone on our hall. It was Annie, my sister. Mother was in a rage; she'd found a pack of Tareytons in Annie's purse. Trouble in Oz, I thought.

"She wants me to drop out of Drama Club," Annie said. She wasn't crying but she sounded on the verge.

"You know she noses around in our stuff! Don't ever leave cigarettes in your purse."

"They were in a Band-Aid box."

"That's the oldest trick in the book, Annie. Parents know about that."

Silence.

"Look, it's probably not a good idea to smoke. I did—you know that—but I stashed my Newports in the garage."

"Oh."

"Buy Clorets too, in case she smells your breath."

"I can't quit Drama Club." Now she was crying. "I'm doing props for *Our Town*, and it starts next week, and—"

"Just tell her they're counting on you, and promise you'll never, ever do it again."

"She says those 'artsy people' are a bad influence."

"I think convincing her you're terribly sorry will work."

Truth was, it might not. It depended on Mother's schedule that week. If she was hosting the garden club or arranging flowers for the altar at St Phillip's, she'd forget about it. If not, Annie would get locked in the tower.

VI.

IT WAS CHILLY FRIDAY morning so I grabbed a sweater and headed off to have breakfast in the dining hall before class. I rarely had more than a cinnamon roll and a carton of milk in the canteen, but today I was starved—and excited. Lewis was coming to rescue me from the zoo. Mr. Monterro had given us the day off to study for his Spanish quiz on Monday, so I only had biology. Then I planned to relax, finish *Intruder in the Dust*, and kill time till five o'clock.

Leaves were raining down on campus from the oak trees; fall was finally coming to Mayville. Crossing the quad I was beginning to feel like a college student—eating breakfast, going to class, having a date. Suddenly Buddy Pippin leaped out at me from behind a bush, scared me to death. Buddy was the dean's son. I'd heard he was "slow" and had seen him around campus. He was short and chubby, always smiling. Close up he looked a lot older than me.

Anna said Buddy loved to listen to the weather report on the radio, then personally broadcast it around campus. He planted himself in front of me grinning, his eyes twinkling. "Sixty-two high, low tonight fifty," he said. "Windy down at the lake." He had a deep, gravelly voice.

"Brrrr!" I said, very dramatic. "Thanks, Buddy!" He chuckled and stepped aside, so I went on my way. When I glanced back he was doing a little jig, talking to himself.

After class I noticed a cop car turning in through the front gates. Sometimes Buddy wandered off and ended up downtown. Eventually a policeman would spot him and deliver him back to Dean Pippin. I figured that was why they were on campus.

I decided to check my mailbox and ran into Martha Stubbs, all bright and cheery, nothing like the ghostly girl who'd floated out of Duke's closet a few days ago. "I talked to my preacher," she whispered. "He said God will forgive me. I mean, for not stopping those girls."

"Where do you go to church?" I asked her.

"Rise and Shine. Pastor Joe said Jesus died for me, so I'll be redeemed."

I had looked up "redemption" and Webster's sent me to "redeem." Now I understood the cross on the highway.

"Did he think we should report Cindy? And the others?"

"We don't have to. God sees all, hears all, knows all."

As it turned out, the cops weren't at Kirkland to bring Buddy home. In front of Thayer Hall, two policemen were packing Barbara Page into the back of their squad car. She wasn't going willingly. Little clusters of girls stood around gawking. "Let go of my arm," Barbara growled. "You guys are crazy . . . you're gonna be sorry. I was set up!" You could hear her motor-mouth still going as they pulled away.

In our room Duke was popping corn for the rush that would come later that afternoon, girls wanting a cheap snack to tide them over till dinner.

"What happened? What'd Barbara do?" I asked.

Duke was low-key as always. "I dunno. They said she shoplifted some jewelry downtown."

"Uh-oh."

"They messed up the bathroom."

It was a wreck in there, everything pulled out of the medicine cabinet. My Pond's cold cream was sitting open on the sink, half-empty. I showed Duke.

"Oh, I saw 'em do that. They fished a ring out of Barbara's jar, and then checked yours."

"I was with Barbara in the jewelry store!"

"When?"

"Monday. What if the cops think I'm a thief too?"

At four thirty I was still keyed up, worried that the police might come to question me. It would be my luck for them to roll in about the time Lewis arrived. I paced like a caged animal for a while, then decided to go downstairs and wait in the parlor.

"Where are y'all going?" Duke asked.

"That's the thing. I don't know. There's nothing to do around here."

"Bowling?"

"Ugh. I hope not." I opened my wardrobe. "Let's see, which mask should I wear?"

"What?"

I pretended to grope around on the top shelf. "What'll it be? Charming Southern belle? Serious Sarah? Jolly, joke-a-minute girl?" I turned to Duke, hands on my hips. "Whaddaya think?"

She scrunched up her face. "You hafta wear a mask?"

"I'm kidding. You know how people put on phony faces sometimes?"

Blank stare.

"What I'm saying is, I don't know much about this guy. I'm not sure how to act around him."

She shrugged and went into the bathroom.

As it turned out, I didn't have to trot out a fake face that night. Lewis was normal, thank heavens, and smart. He knew I would like seeing big city lights. "I'd planned to give you a tour of Mayville," he teased as we headed out of town, "but we're going to Charlotte instead."

"Really? Can we make it back by midnight?"

"No problem. Do you like Italian food?"

"I like all food . . . well, except what they serve at Kirkland."

"Not good?"

"Nothing but starch. Pancakes, rolls, potatoes, corn. Lots of canned corn."

He smiled. "They're filling y'all up for the least amount of money."

We ate at a hole in the wall on the edge of Charlotte. Red tablecloths, candles in Chianti bottles, the smell of garlic in the air. We had cut the small talk a few miles out of Mayville when he asked how I ended up at Kirkland and I told him the story.

"So art's just a hobby."

"I guess. I like to draw but the art degree was Mother's idea."

At dinner he told me he'd had a similar experience with his dad. He had groomed Lewis to take over their peach farm someday, insisted he go to Clemson to study agriculture. "I was relieved when I had to drop out," he said.

"What did you want to do?"

"I didn't know. Still don't."

"Me neither!"

He grinned. "Well, what are you good at?"

"Not much. Drawing."

"OK, what do you *like* to do?"

I thought for a minute. "Read."

He took a sip of wine. "So major in English."

"And do what? I could never teach. I'm too impatient. I mean, if I was fired up about *War and Peace* and my students weren't, I'd wring their little pencil necks." I reached for more garlic bread. "Oops. I'm eating bread when I just complained about Kirkland's starchy diet."

"This is different," he said, snapping up the last slice in the basket. "This isn't Wonder Bread."

It was almost dark when we left the restaurant. Lewis drove on into downtown Charlotte. I acted like a three-year-old. "Look at all the tall buildings," I said, rolling down my window. "And the cars . . . and people."

"Yep," he said. "And noise."

"I love it!"

He found a parking spot and we got out and sat on a bench, people-watching and talking. I told him how hard it was to get used to living in such a small town, how in Atlanta I could drive downtown to the huge Carnegie Library anytime I wanted, or go to a French movie at the Peachtree Art Theater. "I'm sorry. I shouldn't knock Mayville," I said. "You've lived there your whole life."

He shook his head. "You're not hurting my feelings. I went to Atlanta a few times with some of my Clemson buddies. I saw what I'd been missing."

Poor Lewis. I kept jabbering. It was strange being with someone who asked about me. He seemed interested in all of my tales, about Rat Week, getting locked in my wardrobe, the stupid cheers. "I sort of hate myself for not telling them what I thought," I said. "I mean, it was sick to make fun of colored people when they've been getting beaten up by cops and blown up in church."

"I think it's hard to change bigots. They're doing what their parents and grandparents have always done."

"Maybe so."

"At least the Civil Rights Act passed. We're finally making some headway."

I hadn't thought of that. "But I was chicken. Sometimes I hate rocking the boat."

When I shivered Lewis ran back to the car and brought me his windbreaker. He was such a good guy. And nice-looking—about my height, with curly dark hair and eyes the color of root beer. But for some reason I didn't think he was going to be a boyfriend. I enjoyed talking to him, though. He reminded me of my brother, very serious and wise.

I told him about Buddy Pippin scaring me on the way to class, and Barbara getting hauled off in a police car. "I feel like I'm in the Twilight Zone at Kirkland."

"I thought it was a zoo."

"That too."

Barbara Page's parents came and cleaned out her room on Saturday, stripped it bare. Barbara wasn't with them. Wearing my Serious Sarah mask I went to Miss Willis and convinced her I needed to be alone to concentrate on my studies. It hurt Duke's feelings, but I moved into Barbara's room.

Next I walked over to tell Laurie about my date, about Barbara Page's arrest, and how relieved I was the police never showed up to question me. Laurie wasn't there; she'd gone to Myrtle Beach with Anna for the weekend. I wasn't mad, but I couldn't understand why she hadn't mentioned it; I thought we had patched things up. Leaving Laurie's dorm I ran into Cindy Sessions and one of her beauty queen pals on the elevator. She must not have needed the tough girls anymore.

"Hear you had a date last night," Cindy said, poking my arm.

I didn't look at her. "News travels fast."

They both snickered, and when we got out on the first floor Cindy walked with me, asked if I was seeing the guy again tonight.

"Maybe."

"Well, come up to my room when you get in. I'm havin' a party."

Just like that I was supposed to be her buddy? Forget what she'd done to Laurie? Forget she'd slapped me, among other things? "You got any vodka?" I asked, real smart-alecky.

"Yeah, as a matter of fact," she said, "so be sure to come. I want to hear *all* about your new boyfriend."

VII.

I HAD FINISHED *Intruder in the Dust*, so I went to the library to check out something else. I couldn't wait to hole up in my room—alone. Crossing campus I debated whether to alert Miss Willis to the so-called party that night, or slip an anonymous note under Cindy's dorm mother's door. I was desperate to get back at Cindy, but decided to wait. If I ratted on her now she'd know it was me.

Kirkland's library must have been stocked in the Dark Ages. They had only one book by Faulkner, which I'd read. Nothing by Carson McCullers or Flannery O'Connor or Truman Capote, my favorites. No Camus. No Sartre. I almost fainted when I found *Of Human Bondage*. I checked it out and left before the cobwebs engulfed me.

Instead of reading I ended up lying on my bed thinking. I thought about Lewis being twenty-one and still not sure what he wanted to do. He said if his father hadn't died he would've stayed at Clemson learning to run a farm—and hating it. Now he was just biding his time, waiting for something to happen but not knowing what.

Next I thought about Ben, how he'd had the guts to drop out of Vanderbilt and face Mother's wrath. And how Gina Moore packed her bags the minute she knew Flagler wasn't for her. Then and there I decided to emulate Gina and Ben. I would leave Kirkland, go back to Atlanta, and figure out what I wanted to do with my life. I had followed Mother's orders for eighteen years. I'd followed Gina's lead and left Flagler. I'd tagged along with Laurie to a college her parents forced her to go to. No more. I would stop being a little wind-up doll that marched to everyone else's off-key tunes.

It took all week for me to make my exit "the right way." I didn't want to just vanish like Gina and I did when we left Florida. On Monday I wrote my first check. I needed money for the train ticket home. Lewis made the reservation; it was easier than me calling from the dorm. He was disappointed. He'd invited me out for Saturday night. We were going to Spartanburg for a movie and dinner; instead he would be loading me on the *Peach Queen*.

I took a taxi to the bank in town, then walked over to the hardware store to buy a popcorn popper for Duke. Someone had stolen hers while she was at church with Martha. We were sure it was Cindy or one or her goons. I would tell Duke to hide it in my closet when she wasn't using it, leave it there even after I left.

Before catching a cab back to campus, I stopped by the post office on Main Street. I needed to drop off my "revenge" letter. Printed on plain white paper, it read:

Dear Cindy,

This note is from two sophomores. We heard someone telling your dorm mother about some of the stuff you did during Rat Week. We know it was all in fun but Miss Polk might not think so. You are being watched so be real careful.

Your friends

Cindy would be looking over her shoulder, on edge until she graduated in May. It wasn't exactly front page news revenge, but it would shake her up. And so what if she suspected me? In six days I'd be gone with the wind.

I withdrew from Kirkland officially. My permanent record would show WPs—Withdraw Passing—on all of my courses but the History of Western Civilization. In that I got a WI—Withdraw Incomplete. I had cut half of those classes and deserved an F, but we hadn't had any quizzes so no one had a grade yet.

I called Daddy at his office to tell him I was coming home. I promised to bring all my belongings this time, foot locker included. "Tell Mother I'll explain everything," I said. "She won't be upset when she hears my plans."

He agreed, reluctantly, and said he'd be waiting for me at Brookwood Station on Saturday night.

I knew my mother would call. When she did, all I had to say was that the girls here were "not our kind of people," and that I wasn't being "challenged" in my classes. I would tell her I wanted to get a job, live at home for a while, and *carefully* choose a college —with her help, of course.

Daddy must have called her at home as soon as we hung up. Only a half hour later the hall phone rang and I ran out to catch it, my hands shaking. I knew it was Mother; the ring was angry. Right away I got the "I told you so," and "You shouldn't have listened to Laurie," and "You've wasted your father's hard-earned money *again*."

When she finished her speech, I delivered mine. I could hear her take a deep breath. "That's an excellent idea," she said. "Apparently you've come to your senses."

"Yes, ma'am."

"And your timing is fortuitous. You can help me with your sister. She's out of control."

I feigned surprise, promised to do what I could to "rein Annie in" (a popular Catherine expression).

The last thing I did was tell Laurie, which I'd put off till the day before I left. She thought I was nuts. "You've wanted to leave home since eighth grade!"

"Well, as soon as I get my first paycheck I'm renting a little apartment."

"Yeah, sure."

"If I have to do temp jobs, I will," I said. "Seriously . . . and I'll find a roommate if I have to."

Skeptical as she was, she did hug me and wish me luck. She was on Cloud Nine because Roy was coming for the weekend. I suspected she would be back in Atlanta by the end of the semester. This time *she* would follow me.

Rocking along on the *Peach Queen*, I willed myself to think of this as making a fresh start, not returning home in defeat. And I racked my brain for ways to ensure that things happened "my way" when I got there. On the phone Mother had implied that she was too busy to deal with me and my problems, but I knew she was dusting off her wizardess hat and hatching plans for me.

She was in for a surprise. I had always rebelled when she made decisions for me. Every time she pushed Sarah buttons behind her velvet curtain, I fought her. But as the train slowed down on the outskirts of Atlanta, I decided not to do that this time. My mother knew some important people in Atlanta, and I was pretty sure she could pull her magic strings to get me into Emory University next fall. I would major in English lit, not to be a teacher, but . . . I had four years to figure that out. Catherine Claiborne would be thrilled to tell her friends I was studying at Emory, "Harvard of the South." I just needed to make her believe it was her idea.

Stories

Stung

I NEVER PLANNED TO have sex with the bug man. I didn't even have a monthly service contract. All I'd agreed to was a termite inspection. When Joe first showed up in his roach-brown jumpsuit with "Puckett" on the pocket, I didn't notice that he looked like Baryshnikov, didn't look into his swimming pool-blue eyes. Most likely, I was preoccupied, thinking about the chromium canister in his hand with the long dangling nozzle. That cylinder of poison. If he insisted on spraying inside, I would have a growling sinus headache.

"Do you need to come in?"

"No, ma'am, I'll be working outside. We treat the foundation."

"Oh, good. No nasty chemical smells today."

He smiled. "I do need access to the basement."

It's odd how life-changing tiny nuisances can turn out to be. Your neighbor says he's seen termites swarming in your yard. You make the call. The pest control person comes, discovers a problem you didn't know you had. But I'm getting ahead of myself.

Let me first explain who I was the day Joe Puckett lit on my doorstep. Charlotte Ravenel, thirty-seven, daughter of Baird and Virginia Ravenel. Former St. Cecilia debutante from Charleston, South Carolina. Mother of two, PTA president, active in the Junior League. But a year before, my picture-perfect Southern belle résumé had become flawed. My husband of fifteen years discarded me for one of his students, and—oh, you know the story. I was feeling old and ugly, unrecyclable.

I live in Asheville, North Carolina, a lovely small city in the mountains. We moved here in 1992 when Coleman was offered the chairmanship of the history department at the university. I suppose he had a mid-life crisis because soon after we arrived he started riding the ridges with some granola-eating, tree-hugging sophomore. I never suspected a thing, had to overhear one of Coleman's colleagues discussing it in the ladies' room at church.

My two children—Amanda, eleven; Taylor, thirteen—keep me busy so I haven't connected with many women here; only my neighbor Linda. Trouble is, she hounds me unmercifully to get out and meet nice, eligible men. I thought she'd be pleased about Joe.

"Listen, I said when a horse throws you, you're supposed to get right back up and ride. I didn't mean just any horse."

"You're so elitist, Linda. I told you, Joe's got a degree in computer programming."

"I don't buy that. Why would he be working as an exterminator if—"

"You'll love him. You'll see."

It started that day when he came in for the check and saw my new PC. I was fretting about having to set it up and he offered to come back after work to help. That's when I asked why he wasn't working for a computer company. Turns out he was headed from Indiana to Charlotte for a job interview and got side-tracked by these beautiful mountains. Just stopped in Asheville and decided to stay. He'd thought he could get a job here, but nothing panned out. His story made perfect sense and I didn't question it.

I felt comfortable with Joe. We went out for coffee a few times—he'd flit in when he was working in the area—but then I started canceling plans, making a point to be home when I thought he might stop by. I fixated on how I looked: got gold highlights in my chestnut brown hair, ordered workout tapes, bought a black Wonder Bra and a revealing tank top. I never questioned my behavior, just figured I was coming out of my shell.

"You've changed your image," Linda noted. "What, uh, is the look you're actually going for?"

"Sexy."

"Ah, finally ready to get even with Coleman. Good for you. It's about time you got angry at that slime ball."

Linda was way off; I never thought about Coleman. In fact, I could think of nothing but Joe: his incredible eyes; his soft sandy hair, the way it flopped down over his forehead. I went through the motions of cleaning house, cooking for the kids, helping with their homework, but I started forgetting things—meetings, appointments.

Amanda was the first to notice something was wrong. "You need some new pants, Mom."

My clothes were falling off, but I couldn't eat. I sat in the kitchen staring out the window, drinking pots of black coffee. My hands shook and I ran a low-grade fever. My condition didn't improve when Joe and I started having sex, tectonic plate-shifting sex. He would come by on his lunch break and we'd make love. Wild, animalistic love. I'd forget myself, scream out so loud the neighbors must surely have heard. Once, after he left, I stared at myself in the hall mirror, my hair tangled, my face and neck blotchy scarlet. I looked unfamiliar.

Linda dropped by three weeks into the affair. "My god, Charlotte," she said, then stared at me as I brewed a ten-cup pot of Colombian. "I need to meet this man."

"You're the one who's been harping on me to loosen up and have some fun."

"When can I meet him? I'm serious."

I decided on a simple dinner party, just the four of us. The kids would be at Coleman's all weekend and Linda and her oh-so-boring patent attorney husband could meet Joe, see how charming he was. I looked for his number in the phone book; no Joe or J. Puckett in Asheville.

When he buzzed by on Monday, I extended the dinner invitation.

"Uh, I better not." He hung his head. "I'd embarrass you."

"Don't be silly."

"I wouldn't know what to talk to those people about."

He seemed so annoyed I dropped it, but I did ask where he lived. He jerked around from the refrigerator like he'd been stung. "Why do you ask?"

"Well, I wanted to call you about dinner, but you weren't listed."

"Canton," he said, his voice flat.

"You live in Canton? Don't you hate the long commute?"

"No."

He fled like a swarm of hornets was after him. No sex—not even a kiss—just some mumbled excuse about a warehouse to spray.

"He's married," Linda said. "No question about it. Have you ever seen him at night?"

"Well . . ."

"Ever seen him on a weekend?"

I didn't say anything.

"Did you check to see if he's listed in Canton?"

"He's not."

"Look, Charlotte. Face it, his poor frumpy wife got tired of horny housewives plaguing him, so she got an unlisted number. Let's make a trip to Canton. We'll find him, probably in a trailer park with a passel of little Pucketts."

I refused to act like a teenager and go stake out Canton, but I promised to confront him the next time he came by. He didn't come. Days went by and he never showed up. Finally I called Carolina Pest Control. I said I had a black widow spider in my basement, and asked for someone to come out immediately. An hour later, a skinny man whose name patch said "Arnold" arrived. I told him I'd taken care of the problem, sorry for the inconvenience.

It was two weeks before I drove to Canton, crawled up and down streets and side roads, and finally learned from a waitress at the Waffle House where he lived. I'd been busy. I had bagged up my Wonder Bra, the exercise tapes, the scented candles Joe gave me; dropped it all off at Goodwill. I'd dyed my hair brown to cover the highlights, scheduled an appointment with a counselor.

I felt sane, back to my old self, although my stomach fluttered when I pulled into Ridgeview Mobile Home Estates and spotted the van with the giant bee on the roof. It was parked by a trailer with a redwood deck attached, a green turtle-shaped sandbox in the backyard. A sweet-faced bottle blond wearing dangly fish earrings answered the door.

"Listen, I'm so sorry to bother you . . . we just found a wasp nest the size of a Chevy in our attic."

"He ain't home," the blond said, then crumpled into a Lazy-Boy and started sobbing.

"Oh, my, I am so sorry."

She waved her hand like she was shooing flies. "No, no. He's done this before."

I bent down, put my hand on her shoulder.

"He come home, packed up his black suit and Bible and . . ." She reached into her housecoat and pulled out a used Kleenex and blew. "Hit's the chemicals."

"What?"

"Hit's those chemicals he works with. He comes home, says he's breathed in Jesus, and off he goes."

As I stood there, woozy, she told me that Joe was a part-time pastor, that now and then the Holy Spirit grabbed hold of him and he would disappear for weeks. "He's probably calling on folks in hospitals and what-not." she said. "I don't ask. Thing is, see, he always comes home."

The Bridge

FOR MONTHS AFTER her father died, Gwen didn't enter his room, didn't dispose of the clothes and books piled around his bed, or touch the binoculars she'd found under the covers after the coroner left. Then one day she marched in, robot-like, collected his tape recorder and several shoe boxes full of tapes with nothing on them but birds tweeting and twittering. These things she hauled out to the curb in a black garbage bag.

Bedridden after a stroke, Clement Rigg had taken up bird-watching, logging species in a spiral-bound notebook with his one good hand, and recording their calls. Each day when Gwen arrived home, exhausted from shelving books at the Blue Ridge Library, she had to endure her father's incessant chatter about flickers and rose-breasted grosbeaks. Then her second job began: cooking, doing laundry, helping Clement with his bath. At midnight, she would collapse on her bed, knowing that her father's television would wake her at sunup, resonating through the thin walls of their ranch house.

"Are you sure about this one, ma'am?" Earl asked, wiping his brow with his forearm. "This here's a Burford holly."

Gwen sighed. "Yes, Earl, I'm sure. I told you yesterday. Remove them all . . . please."

The old man winced, shook his head. "If'n you don't mind, Miz Rigg, I'm gonna try to get the root ball, see if I can replant it over at the church."

Gwen pursed her lips, shrugged. "Fine," she said and went back inside. She would not pay Earl until the job was done, which he understood; he'd worked for her family for years. She wanted every bush that was close to the house removed, especially the overgrown boxwoods and hollies. They were magnets for the birds that now woke her daily at dawn, singing or squawking for the sunflower seeds she'd stopped putting out since her father died. Of course, she hadn't shared this with Earl; she'd simply said she planned to "re-landscape" the yard.

In fact, Gwen was re-landscaping her life, simplifying, simplifying. She emptied the refrigerator of Clement's junky snack foods, loaded up at the health food co-op, and ate her sparse vegan meals alone in the kitchen. Life was good. The house was silent when she got home, so she could read or just sit and stare out the window at Long John Mountain in the distance.

But when winter came people hunkered down at home, and the library was often deserted, making even Gwen's world too quiet. One morning, for the first time in years, she turned on her car radio on the way to work. She listened to "Morning Edition," then switched to a Christian station where a woman named Mary Lou was blathering about Jesus appearing to her in the laundromat. Gwen laughed for the next mile.

The radio began to entertain Gwen every day on her half-hour trip to and from the library; she even tuned into the local AM station now and then and hummed along with the commercial jingles. Then one day, as she approached the viaduct on the outskirts of her neighborhood, she pictured herself jerking the steering wheel and careening through the guard rail and over the edge. As she had the startling thought, she gripped the wheel, held her breath, and drove on, but once she had crossed the bridge she pulled over. Her mind was racing, her stomach clenched, and she thought she might be ill. She rolled down her window and took a few deep breaths but she had to sit for fifteen minutes before she was able to continue on to work.

Off and on during the day, Gwen would revisit the incident and feel dizzy, but by the time she began the drive home, she had convinced herself that she'd had an allergic reaction to the new muesli she ate for breakfast. And when she sailed over the viaduct that evening with no problem she was sure of it. She had planned to check the ingredients on the cereal box when she got home, but didn't; she simply threw it in the trash.

Unfortunately, the next morning as Gwen approached the bridge, the same image struck her again. In her mind's eye, clear as spring water, she could see her own hand steering the car into the guard rail, and this time she also pictured her car crumpled and smoking on the train tracks below. Today, her reaction was more intense; she gasped for breath, felt she was suffocating, and sat sobbing in the car for a half hour.

"You're not going crazy," Dr. Jeffords said, smiling and looking up from his yellow legal pad. "What you're describing are panic attacks."

Gwen waited for him to say more, but he went back to writing.

"But . . . what's causing them?"

"Stress, most likely."

"I don't have stress."

"Have you thought about getting a roommate?"

"No!" Gwen snapped. She'd answered this man's inane questions for over an hour. Couldn't he just give her a pill?

"Some people find it difficult to live alone. It's an adjustment when—"

"My house isn't set up for a roommate situation. It's not an option."

"Have you considered getting a pet?"

"I'm allergic."

Gwen never went back to the therapist. He was a quack, as far as she was concerned. No decent doctor would sign on with a county employee assistance program. This one was as ineffective as the woman she'd seen after her mother died fifteen years ago. Besides, she was too busy. She had three new volunteers to train at the library, and her car needed work. And for now she'd solved her problem. She was taking an alternate route to work. It took an extra fifteen minutes each way, but she detoured the dreaded bridge.

At Bronson Automotive, Gwen was irritated to see a caged bird behind the reception desk. Why did people feel the need to bring their pets to work? Gwen disliked animals; they drooled, smelled bad, licked themselves in disgusting places. But this bird had an intelligent look in its eyes and appeared to be clean. "What is it?" she asked when the man at the desk finally hung up the phone.

He grinned. "That's Stephan! Isn't he something?" He glanced at the pewter-colored bird in the cage behind him, clearly gearing up to chat.

"What *is* he?" she asked again coldly.

"An African gray."

"Gray *what?*"

"Parrot. He's eight years old. I found him in—"

"I see," Gwen said. "Interesting." She turned and walked back to the waiting area. She hoped they could change her battery in a hurry; she had to be back at work at two. From her black tote she drew a tattered paperback: Conrad's novellas *The Heart of Darkness* and *The Secret Sharer*. She began reading, attempting to shut out the prattle from a flickering TV mounted on the wall beside her. Nothing Montel what's-his-name had to say would be of interest.

"Lovely lady! My, my, look at you. Look . . . at . . . you!"

From where she was sitting, Gwen couldn't see the man at the front desk, but she recognized his voice. Who was he talking to? The bird?

"The rain in Spain stays mainly on the plain." The voice again. Gwen huffed. Obviously the clerk was trying to train the bird to talk. She was tempted to issue a loud shush, as she did many times daily at the library, but one of the mechanics walked in carrying a set of keys and headed for the front desk. Wonderful, she thought, I can get out of here and finish this chapter. She often sat in her car on her lunch hour, reading or resting her eyes. But the mechanic never reappeared and the bespectacled man behind the desk didn't call her.

Gwen drew in a deep breath and then forced it out as loudly as she could. In answer, she received an ear-piercing whistle. "That's it," she muttered. She shot out of her chair and wheeled around the corner, prepared to confront the clerk. He wasn't there. She stepped around the desk, craned her neck to see if he was in the supply room. With that, the parrot began strutting up the wall of his cage. He looked right at her, black eyes glistening. He seemed to be saying, "Watch this," as he climbed up the side and onto the top of his wire cage. There he hung upside down and proceeded to wolf whistle at Gwen.

"Lovely lady. Looov . . . ly laidy!" he shrieked in a perfect rendition of the clerk's voice. "By Jove, I think you've got it!"

Gwen felt foolish. She blushed and turned to go back to her chair when the clerk came in the front door. "It'll be ready in just a minute, Miss Rigg," he said. She didn't respond because the parrot was making a terrible racket. He had scuttled down from his upside-down antics and was pacing back and forth across the floor of his prison.

"Man the torpedoes," he boomed in a commanding voice, much lower than the tone he'd used earlier.

The clerk chuckled. "I think he likes you."

Gwen smirked.

"Most days he dudn't peep till around closin' time. I b'lieve he's showin' off for you. Kinda flirtin', ya know?"

Gwen narrowed her eyes, said nothing, and went back to her seat. Later, as she was writing her check and collecting her car keys, the bird was silent until she glanced at him. "Hello, dahlin'," he said in a sultry voice and winked at her.

From two to four, Gwen shelved books, then reported to the reference desk for the last hour of the day. She detested working reference. Patrons asked her to look up the simplest things, questions they could easily get answered on the Web. Five computer stations would be available, yet they'd come straight to her. Today, however, no one bothered her. Gwen drummed her fingers on the desk and stared at the computer screen-saver. The head reference librarian had scanned in a picture she'd taken in the Bahamas. Tropical paradise. Ha! Gwen thought, recalling the morning's forecast of snow flurries. She clicked on the internet connection, then Googled "African gray parrot."

As a rule Gwen showered in the morning, washed her long straight hair, and let it dry naturally while she boiled water for oatmeal. After breakfast, she would brush her teeth and run a comb through her hair. During the day, she rarely looked into a mirror again. She was not hideous or disfigured; she was plain, a slight, bird-like woman with light brown hair, pale skin, and hazel eyes. Never once in her forty-year life had she sought to make herself remarkable; never had a make-over, experimented with lipstick.

The word "preen" was not in Gwen Rigg's lexicon. But this morning, as the steam cleared from the bathroom mirror, she leaned toward it, studied her face, then stepped back and again scrutinized the image before her. She continued to stare at herself without expression for several minutes, then went about her usual morning routine, which was considerably shorter now that her father was gone. Even taking her new, longer route to work, she still arrived early. On this day she logged on to the computer as soon as she sat down at the reference desk.

"Still reading up on parrots?"

Gwen jumped. "Don't sneak up on me like that," she hissed at Shirley, a young library volunteer who was looking over her shoulder.

Shirley giggled. "They make great pets. My hairdresser's got one."

Gwen said nothing.

"Are you thinking about getting one? You know, they eat fruits and nuts and vegetables—just like us!"

"Researching parrots does not necessarily mean that one intends to buy a parrot, Shirley."

"Well, I—"

"Logically, the two actions do not connect."

"Huh?"

"The *Psittacus erithacus* is the most intelligent of all bird species. That fact interests me. Simple as that."

Gwen scheduled an appointment to have her brakes repaired the following week. The mechanic had said she could put it off for awhile—the pads still had some life in them—but the high-pitched squeaking when it rained was troubling to her. She planned to drop the car off early and call a cab to take her to work. Or, if it was a clear day, she would walk.

Bronson Automotive was dark when she arrived, but a mechanic soon pulled in and opened one of the bays. Then he unlocked the side door and led her into the reception area, switching on lights as he went. Once alone, Gwen paced around looking at the tire displays, the cans of engine oil stacked in pyramids. She needed to get to work, but she wanted to make sure the clerk understood that she wanted only brake pads—nothing else. The man who'd let her in spoke little English; she wasn't about to leave a message with him.

Gwen checked her watch and sighed; she would just have to leave a note. She walked around the counter to look for a notepad. There on the floor was the birdcage, shrouded in tan canvas. My god, she thought, they leave that parrot alone here all night! She had read that without human contact African grays can become severely depressed.

Out the front window cars sped along Mountain Boulevard; rush hour had begun. She picked up a yellow lined tablet and a chewed-on pencil and began to write, but her hands were shaking and she felt dizzy. She could hear clicking in the cage now. She sat down, lowered her head to her knees, and slowly counted to ten. Then she called the library and told the director she wouldn't be coming in.

"I'm sorry . . . I have to leave. I'll have to reschedule."

The mechanic looked puzzled.

"I have to go," Gwen repeated slowly, pointing outside.

The man nodded, though he still seemed confused, and he pushed a button to bring her car down on the hydraulic lift. Heart pounding, Gwen thanked him and backed out, then circled the block and turned into the alley behind the shop. The covered cage was sitting beside the back door where she'd left it. Once she had loaded it into the backseat and was under way—out on the four-lane and headed home—she glanced at herself in the rearview mirror and smiled. She felt powerful, oddly clear-headed and calm, and she knew with certainty that today she would drive home the old way, over the bridge.

The Art of Revenge

WHEN I BELLOWED "goddamn it" and pounded the mahogany end table at the funeral home, I had forgotten that others might be in the building mourning lost loved ones. All I knew was that Judith Gerton Grimes, my stepsister, whom I'd seen only six times in my life, was telling me how my father would be buried.

"Of course, the casket will be open for the visitation," she said.

I looked at my older sisters but they remained mute, perched on matching Martha Washington chairs. Judith paced before us, lecturing, referring now and then to a spiral-bound notepad clutched in her meaty paws. "Judith," I said, in control of myself at that point, "Daddy weighs ninety-five pounds just now. We'd like people to remember him the way he was—rosy cheeks, always smiling."

"This is how it's done in Charleston, Carolyn," she said, speaking to me as if I were gutter trash washed in from Calhoun Street.

My sisters and I had discussed this very issue on the flight from Atlanta, yet they continued to sit silent. "Well, Judith," I said, still somewhat calm, "Cathy and Margaret and I would like—"

"The ladies of Charleston will expect the casket to be open."

"Listen, goddamn it, we are his daughters, and we want it shut!"

That's when my slamming fist set the fake rose medallion lamp teetering on the table and my shrill, un-Charleston-like voice echoed through the halls and brought the little hand-wringing, black-suited funeral director scurrying in.

The following morning we arrived at the funeral home and found the casket open. I was still annoyed with my sisters for their passivity the day before. They'd sat there nodding as Judith outlined every detail of the service at St. Michael's, which she'd planned right down to the hymns we would sing. Again, they weren't reacting, but I couldn't bring myself to close the coffin. I would be haunted forever by the image of Daddy looking hollow, waxen. "Could one of you go close that thing?" I said. "*Please*!"

Margaret said nothing, just sighed and rolled her eyes in that way that says, I am a great microbiologist who cannot abide histrionics; nevertheless, she did what needed to be done.

Daddy grew up in Charleston in one of those stately King Street homes south of Broad Street, a house where both his mother and grandmother were born. When he departed at age twenty-two to work in Atlanta, his mother and her cronies thought he'd taken leave of his senses. Henry Elliott Reynolds Baker, a man with four names and royal blue blood coursing through his veins. Why in heaven's name would he want to move to a wasteland?

Well, he'd earned a degree in architecture at Georgia Tech, and he wanted to use it. He'd gone home to find work but had gotten no offers. I can imagine my crotchety grandmother standing by the fig tree behind 49 King Street, clucking and shaking her head as he departed for Atlanta, that godforsaken Sin City with all the industry and tall buildings and "Nigras" running around acting improperly.

My father stayed in Atlanta for forty years, after marrying my mother. She may not have been a "Charleston girl" but she loved to sail, which made her a perfect life mate in his mind. His mother didn't agree. Forget that Virginia Shelby was smart, pretty, from a fine old Atlanta family. She attended St. Luke's! Unforgivable. In Grandma's opinion the only real Episcopal church was St. Michael's in Charleston. She was never warm to Mother, but the final reckoning came when my sisters and I refused to be presented to Charleston society at the St. Cecilia Ball. After that, she was North Pole cold to all of us.

"Aunt Sally, what if we'd made our debuts over here? Would Judith still be treating us like carpetbaggers?"

She shook her head. "Sweetie, she's a nobody. Don't you worry about her. Everyone knows that buffoon she married is a Yankee, even though he denies it."

Sally and I were peeling shrimp at her kitchen table. "Do you think the Charleston ladies will be scandalized that Daddy's coffin isn't open?"

"I can't imagine where Judith got that notion, Carolyn. I've lived here all my life, and I've never heard of any such rule."

I adore my aunt; she says what she thinks, unlike most citizens of Charleston, South Carolina, capital of decorum. After Grandma died, my father signed over his interest in the King Street house to Sally and her husband, Curtis. My cousins are grown and Curtis died years ago, so it's just Aunt Sally now, rambling around in the big house with three cats and an aging King Charles spaniel. The place is crumbling around her. She says the plumbing is shot and roof tiles crash to the ground daily.

"I'm in the candlelight tour again," she said, sipping sherry from a thimble-size glass. "I'll just turn the lights off, light every candle in the place, and hope no one notices the water stains on the ceiling."

After Mother died my father's childhood friend Louise Gerton came to Atlanta with Aunt Sally for the funeral. "I hope you girls know I adored your mother," Louise gushed. "Whenever she and Henry visited Charleston, I loved seeing her." She fooled my sisters, but I knew she'd come to sink her liver-spotted claws into my bereaved father.

According to Sally, Louise rode the whole five hours with a Styrofoam cooler containing ten pounds of fresh shrimp in her lap. My husband suspected her too. "Whenever a man's wife dies in Atlanta, all the widows show up with Talmadge hams," Jon said. "They're putting their hats in the ring."

"Well, Louise brought shrimp," I said.

"Right, and she knows how Henry loves seafood."

"Jon, Daddy will enjoy her shrimp, but he's not interested in that dried up old hag."

Louise and Daddy married nine months later at St. Michael's, then flew off to Italy for their honeymoon. I drank too much at the reception and threw up all night in Aunt Sally's guest bathroom. The next morning, Jon and I drove back to Atlanta, and from that day forward Louise and her haughty daughter Judith took over my father.

It was one hundred degrees in the shade as we filed into St. Michael's. Judith's son ushered us to the right side of the nave—to the fifth row! She'd filled the first four rows with her friends, and her husband's friends and cousins, and Louise's friends—withered biddies like Louise—and her maid, Hattie, and a passel of total strangers. Daddy's old friends had been seated on the left side and sat white-faced as they saw where we were being steered.

Jon gripped my hand. "Hang on, honey," he whispered, probably afraid of a scene, but I just slithered into that pew like a worm. I may not be a Charleston debutante but I would not embarrass my family. If Aunt Sally had been there, she'd have marched up to Row One and ordered those rubes to move so that we could sit in our rightful places. Unfortunately, she couldn't attend the service; she retains fluid, and her feet were too swollen to fit into shoes.

As the rector began to speak, I glared at the back of Judith's head. I should have seen this coming. Every summer after he married Louise, Daddy rented a house out on Sullivan's Island and invited us all to come. And each time, Judith would trundle out from her home in Mt. Pleasant, plop down in a beach chair, and prattle about the myriad things my father had done for her. Like design and oversee renovations to her house, and help her son get into Georgia Tech. She made it ice crystal clear that he'd become her father.

A year before he died, Daddy called to say he was coming to Atlanta—alone.

"Does he have business over here?" Jon asked.

"Oh . . . you know, he didn't say; I guess we'll find out."

He stayed with us, and we soon discovered his mission: to visit

Mother's grave at Oakland Cemetery. Margaret and Cathy had come for lunch and were complimenting my chicken salad with grapes and pecans when Daddy suddenly produced a diagram of the family plot at Oakland.

"Now, here's your mother." He pointed at a rectangle. "And here's her mother and father. Right here." He held up the paper and moved it around so each of us could see. "Now, this is where I'll be—here, next to your mother."

A grape lodged in my throat.

"I've ordered my headstone. My name and birth date will be carved on it and—"

"Daddy," Cathy said, putting her fork down. "Why are you doing this now?"

He ignored her. "All you'll need to do when I die is get me over here from Charleston." He chuckled. "Get me over here and call Roberts and Shields, and they'll carve the death date."

"Are you ill?" Margaret asked.

He smiled. "No, darlin', but I don't want you girls worryin' about this when the time comes." He took a sip of iced tea and patted his mouth with his napkin. "Now don't you fret."

That's how my father talked. He was a lovely old Southern gentleman. And a lovely old Southern chauvinist, I guess. In his estimation, these were details a man handled, not his girls. Even though two of those "girls" had master's degrees, and one (me) owned an art gallery in Midtown Atlanta.

Not long after that visit he was diagnosed with pancreatic cancer. During the weeks that I flew back and forth to be with him as he lay in the hospital, the disease grinding him down from two hundred pounds to a hundred, I never believed he would die. I didn't believe he'd died when the call came in from Louise. I didn't believe he was dead when I looked at his casket in the funeral home. Now in the midst of singing "O God Our Help in Ages Past," I realized that my father was indeed gone. My sweet daddy was lying in a cold metal box, which Judith had chosen before my sisters and I could even get to Charleston.

I began to sob and choke, and I blubbered and blew my nose in the limousine all the way to Magnolia Cemetery. Yes, Magnolia Cemetery, where Louise—who by South Carolina law could plant her husband any damn where she pleased—was laying my father to rest beside her first husband.

"The mosquitoes were awful out there," Margaret told Aunt Sally. "All through the service you could hear the ladies twittering about Louise burying Daddy next to her first husband. And then you'd hear a slap . . . somebody swatting a mosquito . . . and then more twittering."

"You think it's funny, huh?" I said.

She ignored me, poured herself a glass of Chardonnay.

"Did it dawn on you while you were swattin' mosquitoes that Daddy's wish to be buried beside Mother was not honored? That he's got to lie next to that old lush Walter Gerton for eternity?"

I looked at my aunt; obviously it bothered her. "You know, Louise is deceitful in a way," she said. "She tells people she grew up on Tradd Street, right around the corner. What she doesn't mention is that their house was rented."

"You mean, she's not from an old 'Choll-ston' family?" I drawled.

"Noop. Her parents were from Chester, South Carolina."

"Ha! An outsider!"

"Daddy didn't care," Margaret said.

"I don't think Henry knew what he was doing," Sally said. "He was in shock after your mother died. Then here came Louise with those shrimp."

Thank God my husband's a psychologist. I wouldn't have survived in Charleston without him. He did more counseling with me that week than he does in a month with his bipolar patients. He had to; I'm sure my sisters were upset but they weren't discussing it. Margaret is a squinty-eyed scientist who rarely shows signs of life unless an unusual organism floats under her microscope. As for Cathy, it's a known fact that she's flaky, a musician who's usually off in aerie-faerie land.

They both think I'm too dramatic. Well, I'm an artist; I *feel*. My sisters don't and I've accepted that, but during the funeral debacle I longed for them to show some emotion. Fortunately, just before we left Charleston I did glimpse flickers. We'd walked into Daddy and Louise's house and noticed that the portraits of our ancestors were gone.

"Where are the Theus paintings?" Margaret whispered after Louise had gone to the kitchen to make tea.

"Don't look at me," I said.

"Mother wanted me to have the portrait of Sarah Elliott," she said.

Cathy chimed in. "I'm supposed to get William."

"Those things would look ridiculous in your modern houses," I said.

"Carolyn, hush," Margaret said. "That portrait is mine."

A vein in my neck pulsated. "Wait. You're upset because Mother wanted you to have it? You never said a word when Daddy's wish to be buried in Atlanta was ignored!"

"I was concerned," she said in her usual flat tone. "But it was too late to do anything about it."

Cathy was staring into space at this point, and I could hear Louise coming down the hall. "Well, big sis," I hissed, "you'll have to fight this battle yourself!"

In Atlanta, if you want something done, you can get it done—if you have enough money. You get a famous shyster lawyer and you pay him carloads of money and he gets your job done. Not in Charleston. Let me tell you that in Charleston all the attorneys are arrogant and they all have hyphenated names. They're related to everybody and they hobnob with all these people at the gala balls and they take your money and don't get a thing accomplished for you. They just talk and talk in their "Choll-ston" accents and bill you for every second, phone calls included.

Even after countless meetings with Stuart Reeves-Simmons, Esq., attorney at law, we got not one whit of satisfaction. Seemed we couldn't get Daddy disinterred and moved to Atlanta; we would have to wait till Louise died. And Margaret and Cathy wouldn't inherit the paintings. Our evil stepsister had given them to the Gibbes Museum of Art. She claimed that Daddy "instructed her" to do so. I believe she just wanted her mug in the *Post and Courier*. Caption beneath photo: *Judith Gerton Grimes (left) presents valuable portraits to Gibbes' curator of collections.*

According to our hyphenated lawyer, Daddy hadn't listed the paintings in his will, so there would be no getting them back. Clearly the scales of justice do not tip in favor of foreigners who've trespassed on Charleston's sandy soil.

For months after the funeral I couldn't sleep. When I did drift off I dreamed of Daddy's face just before he died, his vacant eyes and sunken checks. Awake, I obsessed over Judith, wanting to punish her in some way.

"Is it possible you're angry with Henry, but directing it at Judith?" Jon asked.

"Jon, please. I know you worship at the altar of Freud; you think this is all oedipal. But it's not. My father was just too trusting . . . and easily manipulated. I'm not mad at him."

"You think Judith manipulated him?"

"I think she kept him occupied with her stupid little problems. She took him over! Aunt Sally says he spent more time catering to Judith than Louise."

"Okay, honey. Calm down."

"Don't analyze me, Jon; I'm grieving."

He put his hands up, sign of surrender, but suggested I consider talking to someone.

I found a female shrink, a Jungian. She suggested that my depression stemmed from repressed anger. I told her there was nothing repressed about it. And, of course, she wanted to hear about my dreams. Jungians love to dissect dreams. This one almost had an orgasm in her chrome and leather chair when I recounted my dream of beating Judith to a bloody pulp. After four appointments I stopped going. A social worker would have been more helpful. Social workers advise you to set goals and take steps to reach them. Which is precisely what I've now done on my own, and I'm cured. No more nightmares and my appetite's back.

Over time, it came to me that revenge was the answer. I wanted the last word with Judith, and I knew how to get it. I would get the portraits back. All Judith cared about was her standing with "the ladies of Charleston," and she would plummet in their ratings if I could pull this off.

This is the scene I envisioned: A shiny stretch limo cruises through downtown Charleston, down Meeting Street to the Gibbes Museum. I step out in a black Chanel suit, amble in for my meeting with the curator. After brief pleasantries I plunk down a check, a check with lots of zeros, made possible by the sale of one of my own paintings. And I buy back my venerable ancestors in their gilt frames.

"I feel like my old self," I told my friend Jennifer over lunch.

"It's a great fantasy, Carolyn," she said. "But you've got to really do it."

"I know; I have to! But my paintings aren't selling and Jon's practice is down."

"Hmm. Well . . . I know a wealthy widow who's dying for a portrait of her Pekinese."

"Oh, no. You've mentioned that before. I'm not selling out."

"How is that selling out?"

"Next you'll be asking me to do Elvis on velvet."

Never say never. As my income dwindled, I reluctantly did a pastel of the Pekinese. Then a schnauzer and a Siamese cat with cobalt blue eyes. The grandes dames of Atlanta loved the portraits, told their friends. And—this surprised me—I enjoyed doing them; it was a challenge to capture each animal's personality on canvas. I called Jennifer to thank her. "They're all so thrilled to have Kiki and Fluffie and Muffie immortalized."

"Ka-ching, ka-ching, Carolyn. What more can I say?"

My bank account grew, and eventually I saved what I thought would be enough to rescue Sarah and William Elliott from the museum. But on the anniversary of Daddy's death Aunt Sally called. She'd heard that Judith had an inoperable brain tumor.

I was stunned, floored by a rush of conflicting feelings, not the least of which was a sense of myself deflating—the breath swooshing out of me.

"You know what this means," Jon said. "She'll be lucky if she lives through the year."

I sighed. "I guess my plan isn't necessary now . . . really."

"No."

"I'm relieved in a way. You know, Margaret and Cathy don't even care about the paintings anymore; they've let it go."

"And what about you, honey? Are you finished with this?"

"I think so. I think I was finished months ago. I shouldn't have let Jennifer egg me on."

Wisely, my husband didn't comment.

"But I'm actually looking forward to doing more pooch portraits."

He smiled. "What happens when your clients die? Wonder if anyone's kids will squabble over Fido's portrait?"

"Stop it, Jon!" I laughed. But later I obsessed on it a little, thinking about those ladies' cherished paintings in dumpsters, or ending up in yard sales.

Watching for Signs

COUSIN CELIA AND me were spreading peanut butter on pine cones for the birds, and I asked her right out if I brag too much on my boy, Carl. Maybe I do, but he's all I got and he's doing real good in the army, far as I can see.

"What are you talking about, Evelyn? I always have to ask you about him."

"Well, while back I ran into May Ruth down at the mailboxes, and—"

"What'd that biddy say?"

"She asked how Carl was doin' over in Germany. Was he learning to talk with *those* folks; you know, like she talks about *those* Yankees. Anyway, I said I didn't know but he's moving up fast. He's only been in a year and they made him a PF something or other, and now he's going up to carpal."

"Corporal."

"Yep. So now she's taken to calling him 'The General,' real smarty-like."

"May Ruth asked and you told her, Evelyn. That's not bragging.

She's just jealous. Her Billy's been nothing but heartache; everybody in Fletcher knows it."

I'm not much on figurin' why people do things. I've got better to do. Even though my Carl can't see that. He called long distance and I was tellin' him how I tend to this little dog a neighbor's neglecting and he said, "Mama, you need to get a life." It hurt me how he said it, like I'm no-count. He hadn't seen me since he pulled off from that recruiting place last year. I'm so busy all day I'm snoring come eight o'clock. Soon's he comes home, he'll see.

Yesterday I saved a cat. Rodney, cross the way, rode me up to Bi-Lo for milk and we were almost home when I spotted it, right by the Piney Ridge Mobile Park sign.

"Looka there, Rodney," I said. "What in the world?"

He squinted. "What's that cat got on her head?"

"Stop!"

This ol' baggabones stray had got her head stuck in a can. It was the craziest thing you ever saw, a black cat sashaying along with a red Prime Cuts dog food can over her head. I got close as I could.

"Here, kitty, kitty. She can't breathe, Rodney. That thing's sealed down on 'er scruff."

"You better not mess with that cat, Evelyn. It'll claw you good."

I got a hold of her and tugged on that can, but it didn't budge and she took to hissing.

"Help me, Rodney."

"Aw, Evelyn."

"RODNEY!"

He got his sissy-scared self down, left the truck idlin'. I told him to pull on the can while I held onto her. Well, he had to jiggle it around and all but *thuck*, off it came, and that critter tore into his thumb. I can't put down what he said. We went on down to my trailer and I cleaned the bite and gave him a jelly glass of Arlan Jones's apple brandy.

Looked to me like that can was a sign, maybe warning me not to go putting my nose where I shouldn't. I'm not for sure, but I'm praying on it.

Next time my Carl called, I tried to tell him my cat story but he was rattling on 'bout going to Berlin and eating bratwurst. He was proud on account of he used to be a picky eater. Two or three years there he wouldn't touch a thing but saltines and Spam. I didn't say much; I just listened to his voice. It was good to hear him so cheerful.

I got to be gentle on him. Him growing up without a daddy was hard. L.C., his daddy, passed when Carl was four. At first I missed him, but then I got mad. It was his own fault he died. He had this big ol' hernia he wouldn't see to, and one night he was laying too flat in the bed and it cut his wind off. People'd come up after and say, "What'd he die of?" I told 'em hard-headedness, 'cause that's how I saw it. Still do.

I went on working second shift over at Crowson till Carl was seven—Cousin Celia watched him for me—but then I had to go out on disability. Sam Hicks accidently ran the loader over my foot, and it crumpled up some bones like little pretzel sticks. My foot was flat as a floor to begin with, and after two operations it's still not right. Which is why I have to rely on Rodney and Edna next door to get me places.

I never could go back to work but I managed to raise up my Carl pretty good, if I do say so. I wanted to pack us up and move back home to Horse Creek, let little Carl see how folks live fine just on what the Lord provides. But Daddy left the house and the orchard and all to Ed, my brother—there were just us two—and Ed turned around and sold our land to Ray Durrough. Sold him the whole holler. Folks say Ray got greedy, bought him up half of Ashe County.

Ed gave up on Horse Creek on account of one bad winter. It wasn't a fried chicken picnic down here in Fletcher, what with us only having L.C.'s Social Security and my disability. But I clipped coupons and shopped down at Goodwill. I was not going on the dole.

"You and Carl always look best-dressed," my friend Edna says. "I never find a thing at Goodwill."

"You got to be patient, really look," I tell her.

I've been there with Edna. She piddles around in size 14 and then gives up. You need to look in all sizes, 'cause some people try to hide good finds in a different size. Cousin Celia carried me down there last week and I got me an olive green Cabin Creek sweater for three dollars; looked like new.

Edna's eyeballs bugged when she came over that night. Said, "That's J. C. Penney brand!"

"Goodwill," I told her.

Carl's coming home for Christmas, and I'm X-ing off days like a convict. Had to sell a heap of bird houses down at Smiley's Flea Market to get him here; the army won't fly soldiers home to visit like they did when L.C. was in. Folks all over the park keep asking me, "How many now?" Meaning, how many bird houses have I sold.

Rodney builds 'em for me out of scraps from job sites. I paint 'em different bright colors and people snatch 'em up. Tickles me 'cause the birds eat just fine at my plain old wood ones.

Carl put in half the ticket money to get here and I saved up the rest, plus some for the bus. He's got to fly over to Atlanta, and then get off that jet plane and go get on another one to Charlotte, and then catch him a Greyhound to Asheville. Rodney's carrying me up to meet him.

"He's gon' be worn out," I told Edna while we sliced apples for pies.

"He's young, honey. He'll sleep on the plane and be raring to go when he gets here."

"Well, he better not go raring too far! I've not seen him in a year."

By time my Carl came in I was dragging from decorating. Made a red-and-blue banner for out front, said WELCOME HOME PFC SHAW, and strung up colored lights around the front door. Filled up my nine bird feeders and scraped snow off the walkway.

I took Edna's camera to get me a picture of Carl stepping off the Greyhound. First I got a picture of the bus building, then Rodney leaning up on his truck. After Carl came in and I snapped one of him, he bear-hugged me and quick lit him up a cigarette.

"You gon' stunt your growth!" I told him, like I was mad, but then we hooted 'cause he's six-foot-three now. Sprouted up another inch over there. Face filled out too.

Time flew by but we had us a good visit. Cousin Celia fixed a Christmas spread, and Carl kept us howling, telling how those German folks drive a hundred miles an hour over there, highways iced over and all.

Maybe I stuck my nose in, but his last morning at breakfast I told Carl how his high school buddy Cody was studyin' at that tech school in Asheville. "You ought to sign up up there when you get home."

"I'm not sure what I'll do, Mama; that's two years off. Right now

I'm worried about you."

"Me?"

"You can't just sit here painting boxes."

"They aren't boxes. They're bird houses, and you'd not be sittin' here in that chair if it weren't for—"

"What about a home business? Something like stuffing envelopes."

I covered my ears.

"Mama, you need something to keep you occupied."

That's when I went to the kitchen drawer and pulled out the picture. "See that little face down in there . . . in my fern? Day you left, the mama bird flooped the coop. Took 'er other babies but left this one behind."

"And?"

"I had to take care of it. Fed it honey water by hand, and every time it fell out the nest I put it back."

"And it died, didn't it? The mother deserted it because it was sick. It was probably a runt."

"You were a runt, Mister PFC Big Shot, and I didn't leave you to starve to death. You were puny as could be."

"Mama, you can't interfere with nature. That baby wasn't meant to live. Look, we need to find you a real job."

After that I didn't try telling him 'bout saving that cat from the can, or the little lost pug I found a home for. It pains me how he thinks I'm just a-wastin' time.

Since he went back, I been pondering how to make him stop fretting, do something to make him proud. I prayed and prayed on it, and yesterday out in the yard this crow sailed over and dropped a piece of white bread right in front of me. A thick slice, like Wonder Bread. I knew it was a sign, and sure enough, last night the answer popped in my head. I need to start spreadin' up some sandwiches to sell down at Smiley's. I'm down there with the bird houses anyway, and folks' kids always look hungry. A little plop of peanut butter and my blackberry jelly on loaf bread would go good. I can sell 'em cheap but double my money.

Edna says Carl ought not criticize his mama. She saw a man on Oprah advising to be tough when kids don't do you right. I bet that man has a passel of kids, so he can take a chance on one not speakin' to him. I only got Carl, so my case is different. I got my brother, Ed, but he's out in Texas and I haven't seen him in six years. He's put out with me. Won't write nor call. He thinks I ought to have that newfangled E mail. He's ornery like Maw was, even sent me a computer. I'm not plugging that thing in and maybe blowing this place to Mount Pisgah.

Anyway, sandwiches are a better way to help folks than lickin' envelopes. I know it in my toes. I just hope my Carl takes to the idea.

Choked Up

WE NEVER LOOK at each other anymore when we eat, Eve thinks. We used to stare at each other, giggle. Back then he didn't wolf his food. Or did he?

Kenny and Eve are eating lunch at the Busy Bee Café, which isn't busy, halfway between Atlanta and St. Simon's Island. Kenny hates fast food and has driven miles off the interstate to find a non-McDonald's. Eve nibbles on a salad, stopping now and then to spear a carrot or bit of cauliflower with a bent fork. Kenny is attacking a slab of meatloaf smothered in onions and gravy.

"How much farther is it?" Kenny asks, squirting his mound of cottage fries with off-brand ketchup.

"A few hours, maybe three."

He eats too fast, she thinks. His bites are too big and he forgets to wipe his mouth. She toys with a metal ashtray on the table, begins twirling it.

"Should we go to the beach as soon as we get there?" he asks.

"Let's play it by ear." Eve says this like a teacher addressing a young student. She is chewing carefully, patting her lips with her napkin after every few bites. She glances at the only other person in the restaurant, a scrawny guy with dreadlocks, then out the window. A young couple has turned into the parking lot, and she squints to see what they're doing. Studying a map, it seems. They nuzzle, kiss, pull back out into the road.

Eve's stomach knots and she puts down her fork, tries to remember the turning point, the moment in time when she and Kenny stopped acting like that. What day on seven years of calendars would be circled in red? She spins the little tin ashtray now, so hard it flies off the table. Kenny bends to retrieve it, a tiny tail of onion dangling from his lip. "If Hoke brings his kid to the job site again, Larry's gonna punch him out," he says, clipping off the onion with an enormous bite of fries. "He tripped on the kid's skateboard yester . . ."

He stops mid-sentence, stares over Eve's head toward the cash register, worry grooves appearing between his eyebrows. She turns to see if someone is holding up the restaurant. Nothing. Just a woman stacking buns on a shelf. Annoyed, she looks back at him. A gurgling sound is coming from his throat.

He shouldn't talk with his mouth full, she thinks, then gets concerned. He's clutching the table now, back arched, eyes wide. "Are you okay? Can you breathe?" Eve leans toward him, thinking of Mrs. Lawson, her mother's friend who choked to death in a steak house.

He shakes his head—not side to side, not up and down, more like a quarter circle. Was that yes or no? she wonders, her mind scrambling. The Heimlich maneuver. Can I do it?

"Are you getting any air?" she asks, frantic.

Kenny grabs the table again, stretches his mouth open even wider—it's now a giant "O"—and rears back in his seat. A voice in Eve's head directs her: Grab him around his stomach! Bend him over!

Kenny is frozen now, eyes squeezed shut. But just as Eve jumps to action, knocking over her iced tea, he slumps in his chair and lets out a swooshing breath. "I'm fine," he says weakly, breaking into a broad grin.

"My god, you scared me to death! I couldn't tell if you were nodding or shaking your head when I asked you . . . when I asked if you were getting any air." She can feel adrenaline spurting into her stomach. "*What happened*?"

He smiles sheepishly, shrugs. "I don't know, I jus' had a little piece of potato caught in my throat."

"In your throat? It wasn't in your windpipe?"

"No, it kinda got stuck. I couldn't get it up and couldn't get it down."

"Well, why didn't you drink something?"

When he shrugs again, Eve snatches her purse off the floor and charges out of the restaurant.

"I can't take this. I swear, I'm such an idiot. Why, oh why, did I plan this trip?" Eve is pacing the parking lot, trying to dispel the adrenaline. She has speed-dialed her friend Julia on her cell phone. "He's testing me. It's so obvious!"

"Wait a minute, Eve, what are you saying? You think he was faking?"

"He knows we're done—over, end of story."

"But I don't get how that was a test. Wouldn't any decent person help somebody who's choking?"

"I swear, Julia . . . if you'd seen him . . . he's trying to see if I still care."

"Look, why don't you just tell him what you think?"

"What I think is he's been acting comatose since we talked about separating. And now this! It's not going to change anything, Julia."

"Maybe you shouldn't have planned a trip. I mean, this vacation might give him false hope."

"I don't know, I . . . uh-oh, here he comes. Gotta go."

"Do you want that pillow out of the trunk, baby?"

Eve says nothing, just stands by the passenger side door waiting for Kenny to unlock it.

"The little one you brought for your neck?"

When she doesn't answer again he scratches his head and, whistling, clicks the remote door opener to let her in.

Eve looks straight ahead as they pull out on the highway, and for the next eighty miles she responds to Kenny's chit-chat with grunts, uh-huhs and uh-uhs. The specter of the restaurant incident crowds the seat between them, a hulking presence, and as she always does Eve dissects the scenario in her head, replaying it over and over. She knows Kenny isn't thinking about it. That would not be his nature, which is why she was drawn to him in the beginning. His carefree, non-analytical temperament counteracted her tendency to obsess, softened her sharp edges. How ironic that his light-hearted worldview is now the very thing that annoys her most.

By the time Kenny stops for coffee at a Jiffy-Mart outside McRae, Eve is convinced that he was testing her—but not consciously, which makes it a lesser offense. Getting back into the car, he stumbles, flips scalding coffee on his leg. "Aww . . . ahhh!!" Eve glances at him, stone-faced. How unoriginal, she thinks. That one's already been done.

Nevertheless, her eyes are drawn to Kenny's leg, and she is relieved to see as he swabs up the brown liquid that his shorts have taken the hit; the flesh isn't even red.

"Are you okay?" she chirps, then pats his leg.

Once they're under way again, Eve experiences a wave of nausea, but she pops in an Adele CD and hums along with it. After the first cut, she finds herself considering what Julia said about giving Kenny hope. Maybe this whole relationship was built on her own false hope; clearly her initial belief that a blues guitar-playing carpenter and an anal-retentive accountant could make it as a couple was a pathetic fantasy.

On St. Simon's Island, as they pull into the black wrought iron gates at The King and Prince, Eve finally looks at him. "Why do we keep kicking this horse, Kenny? It's been dead for a while, don't you think?"

No reaction. His right nostril may have twitched, but she can't be sure. "Honey," she says softly, "we've got to talk before we go back. Really. Not about my little habit of clicking my fingernails, how it bothers you, or how your beer slurping drives me insane. You know it's more than that. Listen, I don't want to be alone either, but . . ." Suddenly she can't speak; her throat has closed and her mouth has filled with metallic-tasting saliva.

Kenny sits for a moment, then draws up as if he's waked up with a start. "I'll run in and get the key," he says, his voice strong, assuring. "I hope our room's right on the beach!"

She stares ahead, eyes unfocused, but when he gets out of the car she turns to watch him as he bounds up the steps two at a time. At the top he stops abruptly, drops to his knees clutching his chest. His agonizing groan reverberates off the hotel's thick glass door. She leaps from the car, tears up the stairs to the now unmoving heap. A bellboy has rushed out, along with others who have heard the howl.

"Stand back," the bellboy orders. "Please. I know CPR." As he rolls the heap over, grabs at the shirt to rip it, Kenny's eyes flutter open.

"What? What the . . . ?"

"Are you all right, sir? Sir? Are you all right?"

"What? Oh, fine, fine. Heartburn, I guess. I don't think . . ."

Eve slaps her hands over her ears, turns, and descends to the car slowly, as if she's under water. The engine coughs and sputters when she cranks it, but just as she begins to cry, it catches. Thick black and blue smoke billows from the tailpipe as she wheels out, heads north to the causeway.

More than an hour has passed when Eve returns, pulls under the porte cochere at The King and Prince. Kenny is sitting on the steps beaming. "We got it, baby," he shouts. "We got a room lookin' right out on the beach!"

Shame on Me

KIDS CALLED ME Lump-Lump in school 'cause I was pudgy, and after I got married and had babies I got bigger and wider and mushier. But now I'm a beanpole. I lost sixty-six pounds on Dottie's Diet. I know I ought to be right thrilled that Dottie's gotten so famous, but I'm not. I'm scared folks are gonna find out what I've done. It's weighing so heavy on my heart, I've started snackin'. But I'm getting off track, so let me go back to before Dottie invented her diet.

No one outside Georgia ever heard of Hahira, my hometown. That's pronounced Hey-Hi-Ruh. See, we're just a little sneeze on Highway 41 between Adel and Valdosta. And when the interstate got finished, people on the way to Florida quit passing through. Loads of our stores shut down.

But as I said, that was before Dottie's Diet put us on the map. Now we got TV people with ponytails hauling in here in giant vans from New York City, and CNN reporters roarin' down from Atlanta. Our population's done shot up from five hundred to four thousand twenty-two! Everybody wants to get skinny and they want to know Dottie's Diet secrets. We could tell 'em about it on the phone, but, no, they think they need to move to Hahira. Dottie says maybe they think there's something special in our water.

We got an out-and-out real estate boom going on. And local folks who lost a heap of weight are all the time gettin' interviewed on TV. Like our mayor, Jimmy Bob Potts. He used to take up two seats at the church, but now he's downright lanky.

Sounds great, huh? Well, it is now. But this fall, when Dottie's diet centers open up all over the place, things are gonna blow up like the A-bomb down here. I'm just scared silly they'll find out what I been doin' and hang me up by my toes.

It's not like I planned it. It just happened. After I lost my sixty-six pounds, I was helping Dottie weigh people every week. (We used to meet at her house back then.) One afternoon this cute little ol' gal, Ivy, had one more pound to go to hit her perfect weight, which Dottie has a chart for. Anyway, Ivy came in right perky and proud, said she hadn't cheated all week. Honey, she just knew she had it made. Well, she got up on the scale and I saw she'd gained a pound. Ivy couldn't peek 'cause Dottie rigs it up so's only the weigh-in person can see the number.

I'm confessin' right now—out loud—I lied. I didn't have the stomach to tell Ivy the bad news, so I told her she'd lost a pound, and I tooted the little whistle Dottie keeps on the desk. Everybody clapped and came over and hugged Ivy, and after the meeting we celebrated with frozen blueberry push-up pops (low-cal treats Dottie thought up).

I know it was wrong and I shouldn't have kept doing it. But I did. Every week I told one of the ladies she lost pounds she really didn't, and something right cuckoo happened. The folks I fibbed to got thinner and thinner, even when the scale said their pounds were goin' up!

Then the men started coming in, and I did the same thing with them. If they gained five pounds, I told 'em they lost five; then lo and behold, the next week they'd come in with their belts cinched up two or three more notches.

I tell you what's truth: it's some kind of miracle. Oh, Dottie's diet's real good—lots of fresh vegetables and fruits and all—but we got people dropping down four and five dress sizes in no time. Ladies who been totin' around that fat all their lives.

Trouble is, I can't be in Minneanapolis and Shy-Anne and Knocksville all at the same time. When folks around the U. S. of A. start weighing in come September, I don't know what'll happen. I just pray to the good Lord this magic keeps on goin'.

The Decision

THE SUN APPEARS for the first time in weeks. Dillon surveys the wreckage in his studio: the piled newspapers and paint brushes, litter of coffee cups, grease-stained takeout bags. How can he let Bonnie Braithwaite-Banks, grande dame of the art world, come here? He's not sure he wants her to see his work anyway. If she likes it, offers him a show in a Manhattan gallery, he'll have to attend the opening—at the very least—and god knows what else. Interviews? Speaking engagements? His ancient Honda would never make it. And what if she hates it, or doesn't get it, or thinks it's ho-hum? He'll have to hang himself. He looks up, searching for a possible place for the rope. Does he have any rope?

When Dillon's artist friend Hal called to say he wanted to bring BBB out—she was going to be in Asheville for a day or two—Dillon lied, said he wasn't sure he'd be in town.

"Well, let me know tomorrow. Her schedule's tight."

"I don't know, Hal. I—"

"Unless you've got an audience with the Pope, you need to let her see your stuff, buddy. She could be your ticket to ride."

Dillon wanted to believe him. The woman had gotten Hal's abstracts into a dozen galleries, not to mention two one-man shows in New York and Boston. "OK, man, I'll get back to you."

Jerry-rigged to the back of the old guest house that serves as Dillon's studio is a flat-roofed screened porch. On it, a lone metal chair faces what was once a grassy, flower-bordered yard and the hardwood forest beyond. Other than the chair, there is no furniture, unless the stacked, rusty paint cans could be considered a side table.

The crickets and spiders that have resided on the porch all summer, this foul summer of rain and mildew and rotting foliage, suddenly scatter across the concrete slab floor. Dillon has opened the door and is slinging his studio detritus onto the porch, including great bundles of textiles—a moldy blanket, a gray towel streaked with burnt umber, chartreuse boxer shorts with smiling Day-Glo skulls. Out objects fly until Dillon finally reaches the stratum of small items and begins sweeping them out. Spent paint tubes, squeezed and twisted into obscene shapes, pizza crusts, unopened mail.

A breeze has picked up and the sun, a fuzzy yellow disk overhead, illuminates the studio. Dillon stops working, runs his hands through his shoulder-length hair, and glances up at the skylight. Puffy clouds drift across the square of glass, several in the shape of giant faces, two that Dillon recognizes. One is jolly St. Nick, his fat round face framed by silvery locks that curl down around his cotton-batting collar. Dillon purses his lips, unwilling to acknowledge the sign from the art gods that Santa Claus is hovering over his house.

The other image in the passing cirrus gallery is unmistakable; it's Dillon's Uncle Fred, grinning down at him, one drunken eye shut—like he's winking. Dillon cocks his head back and howls. His uncle is the one family member who believes in his work, feels sure he can make it in what he refers to as "the big-time."

His sweeping complete, Dillon aims the broom like a javelin, launches it onto the porch, then slams the metal door. A wall of the studio is lined with floor-to-ceiling cabinets. He strides toward them; beneath his cargo shorts the Bengal tiger tattooed on his right hip moves boldly along with him. He starts at the end of the row and opens the first cabinet, pauses, then steps to the next and yanks it open. And the next and the next. His tiger doesn't seem to know whether to crouch or spring.

The cabinets house all of Dillon's paintings—every stroke from his brush over the last nine years. No one has laid eyes on them but his friend Hal, and Uncle Fred, of course. Both men have harped on him to show his work, at least let others see it, but he has obdurately resisted. In art school negative feedback from instructors made him feel worthless and he became blocked. Their praise, on the other hand, left him anxious that they'd expect similar work from him, which he might not be capable of producing. Either way, he froze, couldn't function for weeks.

Dillon imagines it would be no different with THE Bonnie Braithwaite-Banks. Regardless of her reaction to his work, he would be incapacitated, forced to continue eking out a living as caretaker here on the old Campbell estate. And what if Ezra Campbell's sole heir, who lives on the West Coast, suddenly decides to sell the place? Then what? Wait tables? Panhandle on Biltmore Avenue?

Despite this line of thinking, he begins pulling out his paintings, some framed, some not; for help with this task he'll need the London Symphony. Orff's *Carmina Burana*, top volume. Dillon has no surround sound, no Bose; his boom box from Goodwill will have to do. The fake paneled walls of the studio do not reverberate with full-throttle bass, the way he likes his music; nevertheless, he works on, carefully carries each canvas to the perfect spot in the room and props it against the wall.

By mid-afternoon the studio is ringed with artwork. As if programmed, the tape player clicks off after "O, Fortuna" at the moment he steps back to view his handiwork. Every painting is displayed to its best advantage, and in the center of them all is Dillon's pièce de résistance, a hinged wooden triptych he calls "Shrine to the Black Madonna." Even in fading light its deep, rich colors, especially the blood red, pulsate with life. And the gold-leaf halo ringing the Virgin's head seems to expand until an aura glows around the entire shrine.

The light is coming up, but not like yesterday; today will be muggy and overcast. Dillon sits on his porch, staring at the woods. His face is blank, as blank as the new canvas that lies in the trunk of his '99 Honda. A brown rabbit emerges from the forest and moves toward the porch, toward Dillon, then stops, ears twitching. When he hops away, he veers off to the driveway and then down toward the road—purposefully. Dillon has watched the rabbit countless times on mornings like this, nibbling at greenery around the edges of the yard. He's never shown any interest in crossing the road. Dillon believes he'll turn back.

At least five minutes pass but the rabbit does not reappear. Dillon rises from his chair and picks his way through the minefield of trash to a place that allows him a full view of the driveway. There's the little guy, poised at the end of the gravel drive looking at the wide asphalt road.

Ha! You can't do it, can you, mate? Dillon thinks. He smiles, pats his shirt pocket, then pulls out a crumpled cigarette pack. Two left. He lights one with his old Zippo, a gift from Uncle Fred, and decides to gamble. If the rabbit crosses the road, heads off across that vast, treeless expanse of lawn toward the Campbell house, he will let BBB come. If not, he'll call Hal and tell him "no go." The queen of high art will have to leave Appalachia empty-handed.

Dillon smokes and watches, snickers when the bunny sits on his haunches and continues contemplating the highway. After a few minutes Dillon kicks aside a brown apple core with the edge of his sandal, then bends down to rub out his cigarette on the concrete. When he stands the rabbit is gone! His heart pumps; he squints, scans the rolling lawn across the road. Nothing. He spins on his heel and surveys the backyard, the yellow-brown patches of grass and ragged garden. No sign of Peter Rabbit. He's vanished, and Dillon has no way of knowing whether he crossed the road or hopped back to the forest.

It happened so fast; he'd turned away for—what? Ten seconds?—to butt out his cigarette. The goddamn cigarette. Perhaps he'll offer up the last one to the Black Madonna, light it for her and set a can of varnish nearby, let the whole freaking place go up in flames. But he doesn't, nor does he search for rope in the tool shed out back; instead, he goes inside and picks up the phone.

Memory of Fire

IT'S UNMISTAKABLE, that strong sulfur smell. Matches. Wooden kitchen matches. I'm jogging in my neighborhood and spot two boys crouched over a pile of crumpled paper. From their furtive glances it's clear they're up to something. One tow-headed boy reminds me of my childhood pal Tommy Sims, which immediately gives me a lump in my throat.

Tommy and I were only six or seven when we burned down three acres of woods in our suburban Atlanta neighborhood. We'd built an elaborate fort out of old bamboo porch blinds, then camouflaged it with pine straw. To us, it was paradise. Problem was, it was dark inside, so we filched candles and matches from our respective homes. The rest, I'm sure, was detailed in the incident report.

After the fire engines pulled away late that afternoon, I was seated in our living room and given what my father called "a good talking to." As he lectured in his soft Tidewater accent I tried to listen, but I could hear Tommy's wails from five houses away. He'd told me about his "scoldings," so I knew his father was beating him with a thick black belt.

Young as I was, I was aware of the disparity between the scenes at my house and Tommy's. We'd been equal partners in crime, yet there I sat, high on my side of the scales of justice looking down on him—flat on the ground. And in that instant I experienced what were likely my first conflicting feelings. I felt sorry for Tommy, very guilty, but relieved not to be in his shoes.

S.O.S.

ALL YEAR WE WATCHED—and listened—as Henry Eklund clunked along, clomping his huge brick-like shoe, which was attached to steel shafts that braced his bad leg. My mother said polio had withered Henry's leg, left it shorter than the other one, that the big shoe made his legs even. Still, he had a terrible limp and cruel boys teased him in the lunchroom.

"Click-stomp, click-stomp," they'd chant, out of earshot of teachers, of course. This was a private school, and nice private school children didn't deride their peers. That was behavior you'd expect from kids in public school, which is why my parents had refused to let me attend one.

Those ill-mannered boys had little opportunity to taunt Henry in our classroom. Mrs. Pierce was as stern as the black lace-up shoes and gray suits she wore, and we were terrified of her. When I bring up her image today, decades later, I can still see the wart on her sunken cheek, and the deep lines that radiated out like spokes around her mouth, probably as a result of her lips being pursed for years. If you raised your hand to go to the bathroom she'd ignore you, or if she acknowledged you and you asked to please be excused, she'd tell you to hold it. She said second grade was very serious business; we dare not miss a thing. One day, Tony Liberto wet his pants—he'd never even raised his hand—and then sat there and sobbed because we were all staring at the puddle beneath his desk; but nobody laughed.

I remember only a few more things about that year, like Skipper Willingham getting his finger caught in a broken bar on the jungle gym. They rushed us inside, but from the window we could see grownups huddled around him. Skipper didn't come back for a while, and when he did the tip of his index finger was missing.

As for me, I brought little toys from home every day to butter up my friends and possibly acquire a few new ones. I was running out of toys and getting panicky on the day Henry Eklund tried to throw himself into the stairwell from the third-floor landing.

Henry and I were at the end of the line snaking down to lunch. I stopped at the water fountain, then turned to find him poised on his good leg and using both hands to hoist his big-shoed foot over the railing. Though I was only seven, I understood right away what he was doing. I grabbed him around the waist, planted my feet, and screamed "Help" over and over, louder than I'd ever yelled. My howls echoed through the empty hallway and down the cavernous stairwell. And now as I look back on that incident, which rendered me a hero of sorts, I realize I was not calling out for help just for Henry.

Where There's Smoke

MY STRAWBERRY BLOND hair looked pea green beneath the fluorescent lights in the girls' restroom at Ashburn Academy. Annoying, but not a serious problem. What caused me real angst were the horrid things that happened to me there. Like finding out that Chip Pittman was cheating on me. Like having my sixteenth birthday ring stolen. A gift from my parents, it was my first real piece of jewelry—a beautiful sapphire set in gold. Yes, it was my fault I left it on the basin, but not my fault that some little minx snapped it up and kept it.

But those events pale in comparison to the scene in that bathroom one lovely spring afternoon decades ago. I'm not referring to something trivial like hearing I didn't get picked for the pep squad. I'm talking criminal offense.

A classmate, Beth Ann Beadle, was the perpetrator. Everyone called her The Beetle—to her face, and not in a fun, joking way. Beth Ann wasn't stupid or ugly or dowdy, none of those things that make high school kids unpopular. What made her hated, despised actually, was her holier-than-thou attitude, combined with the fact that she was a RAT in capital letters, a tattletale to the nth degree.

If you snuck food into the library, or talked in chapel, or passed notes in class The Beetle called you out on it. And if you didn't change your ways immediately, she reported you.

"Who named you chief of police?" my friend Deborah asked her one day in biology.

"We've got an honor system here, in case you haven't noticed," Beth Ann answered in her nasal, know-it-all tone.

"She's pathetic," another girl chimed in. "Don't waste your breath on a bug."

Beth Ann Beadle just rolled her eyes and swished off to fifth period Latin, her nose in the air. She didn't seem to mind having no friends, but I think the constant heckling eventually took its toll—a bit like Chinese water torture. In gym, in the cafeteria, catcalls rang out the minute she entered. "Rat fink!" "Beetle brow!" And when adults weren't within earshot, "Bitch." Some girls made oinking sounds at her (her nose was a bit porcine) or moved in close and coughed in her face. "Oh, excuse me. I didn't see you!"

You can't bully someone like that without consequences, and I happened to be in the path of the scorching lava when Beth Ann finally erupted.

It was a warm, breezy day in April, and we'd opened the crank-out windows in the bathroom. Three of my friends and I packed into a stall and lit up our Salems. Smoking gave me a headache, but in those days I did whatever it took to be in with the in-crowd. Joanie and Nan stood on the toilet seat, one on each side. Deborah and I scrunched in against the side walls.

Smoke was billowing up from our little lounge—as of course it would with four people puffing away—when the door opened. Joanie and Nan ducked so their heads couldn't be seen. We ditched our cigarettes in the bowl—*ppffftttt, ppffftt, ppfffft*—and didn't move, terrified it was a teacher. After a minute or two of complete silence, I peered through the crack and saw Beth Ann combing her hair. "It's just The Beetle," I whispered.

"Oh good grief," Deborah said, really loud. "Somebody call pest control. There's a huge insect in here!"

"Looks like a cockroach to me," Joanie said.

We all laughed and started chatting again. A toilet flushed, then suddenly a ball of fire the size of a human head came rocketing under the door of the stall. We tried to scramble to the back wall, flatten ourselves against it, but flames were shooting up and we were shoving and shrieking. Somebody finally got the door open, and we spilled out of the booth. Everyone but Deborah. She had gotten up on the toilet, then jumped down on the burning orb—now the size of a tennis ball—and stomped it out.

Nan's twin sister, Ann, rushed in as the last flicker was extinguished. "Beth Ann just blasted out of here," she said, surveying the charred mess on the floor. "What happened?"

No one answered; we were coughing and checking our legs and skirts, and trying to calm down. Eventually we picked through the debris, and it became clear that a roll of toilet paper had been set on fire, then kicked under the stall. It was a miracle that our school uniforms, full-skirted cotton dresses, had not ignited. We didn't tell anyone what happened. How could we without implicating ourselves? From that day forward, none of us teased Beth Ann again; we did not want our names on her hit list.

Ten years later, my husband and I were invited to his boss's house for a dinner party. That night, when his wife answered the door, my stomach clenched. Dear God . . . Beth Ann Beadle! I had never led the pack that preyed on her in high school, but since I never stepped in to defend her, I'm sure she despised me as much as she did the others. Now she pretended not to recognize me, although her eyes betrayed her. And I went along. "So nice to meet you," I purred. We were oh so civilized! But throughout the meal, I tasted each tiny bite cautiously, wondering how much rat poison it would take to kill someone.

The Kindness of Strangers

MY FRIEND PAM and I were sixteen when we ventured into an exotic new realm—dating college boys. Not such a great thing, as it turned out.

We were ever so mature, far too cool for boys in our class. So when Pam's older sister fixed us up with two Phi Delts at Georgia Tech, we happily left sock hops in the school gym behind.

Andy and Jim first met us after school at the Varsity, Atlanta's famous curb service joint near the Tech campus. The term "fast food" wasn't used in the early 1960s, but orders at the Varsity arrived at your car before you could say "chili dog."

The guys were cute, but I was disappointed that they were from Alabama. I'd longed for a boyfriend from up North. (I love foreigners.) They treated us to fries and shakes, asked us out for Saturday night, and told us to dress up.

"For a party?" Pam asked. "At the frat house?"

They looked at each other and grinned. "We'll pick you up at eight," Andy said.

"What'll I tell Mother?" I whined on the way home. "She'll never let me go out with a nineteen-year-old."

"Just spend the night with me," Pam said. Her dad was in California on business, and her mother would be sloshed by dinnertime. She did enjoy her "toddies," according to Pam.

I wore the only thing I owned that seemed sophisticated, a dress with a straight skirt and a wide belt. It was rust-colored, which I thought complemented my auburn hair.

"Oh, no," I mumbled, standing in front of Pam's full-length mirror. I hurried into the bathroom where she was applying eyeliner, the cake kind you had to wet and paint on like watercolor. "When I cinch in this belt, the end of it sticks out."

Pam held up a finger to indicate "just a minute," went off down the hall, and came back with a straight pin. "Here."

"What's that for?"

She rolled her eyes and jammed the pin into my fabric belt at an angle. Voilà! No more flapping belt.

We had no idea how we would pair up that night, but I wanted Andy and she wanted Jim. Thankfully, we were never attracted to the same kind of guy.

When the boys arrived at eight thirty, not eight as promised, Andy came to the door. If we'd been at my house, my mother would've grilled him on his family tree back to the *Mayflower*. As it was, Pam's mom was conked out cold on the sofa in front of *Truth or Consequences*.

At the car Andy motioned Pam to get in the back seat. She glanced at me and scowled. Andy had chosen her. Why, oh why, did the tall guys always prefer petite Pam, leaving five-foot-nine me to the sawed-off ones?

I slid into the front seat with Jim. "OK, ladies, big night," he announced as we pulled away from Pam's house. "The Isley Brothers are in town."

"You're kidding!" Pam shrieked, leaning forward to poke me in the shoulder. We'd been practicing The Twist to their hit record "Shout" for weeks.

Andy said, "They're at the Peacock."

"What's the Peacock?" I asked, then froze when he said it was a black nightclub downtown on Auburn Avenue.

"They get all the hot groups," Jim said. "The Supremes, the Tams, Martha and the Vandellas."

"And they let white kids in?" Pam asked.

Jim shrugged.

If my parents get wind of this, I thought, I'll be grounded till I'm forty-five.

The flashing neon sign over the marquee read "Royal Peacock Social Club." As we scaled the narrow staircase I imagined the Peacock patrons cold-shouldering us, or worse, glaring at us for crashing their club. But inside everyone smiled and nodded. Two men came up to Jim and shook hands; turned out he'd booked their band to play at a Phi Delt party. A guy with sunglasses and a black silk shirt led us to a table close to the stage. And when we ordered bourbon and Cokes, no one checked our IDs.

After a few numbers by some local group, the famous brothers strutted out in glitzy bright-blue jackets. Everyone whooped and whistled; no more sipping drinks, chatting in low voices. By the end of their second song, we were all out of our seats, clapping and gyrating in the aisles. And when a wiry little band member amped up the sound, the crowd went crazy.

Burly bouncers tried to restore order but failed, so when Jim shouted, "Let's go out to the lobby," I nodded and followed him. Unfortunately, people were whirling and crashing into each other out there too. We had no choice but to join in.

I'd had only a few swallows of bourbon and Coke but was tipsy enough to twist like a corkscrew—up and down to the floor—belting out "You make me want to shout" along with the famous band.

No one seemed to care that more people had wandered in off the street, cramming us together like the canned smoked oysters my parents ate with cocktails. In fact, there was very little room for me to collapse when my right leg suddenly separated at the knee—one bone going one way and one the other. At least that's what Jim told me later that night. I can't be sure since I fainted.

When I came to in the ladies' room, a plump woman in a red satin dress was fanning me with a newspaper. "You gon' be all right, honey," she said. I was stretched out on a long couch and she pulled up a chair to sit beside me. "Let's loosen that belt so you can breathe." She yanked out the straight pin and unhooked the buckle.

"Hold this, Gladys," she said, handing the pin to a woman perched on the arm of the sofa.

Several other women gathered around. "What happened?" one asked.

"I don't know . . . I slipped, I think. The floor was sticky."

"Girl, you just had one too many," a woman with a yellow flower in her hair teased.

"No, no, I . . ."

I couldn't finish because I'd moved my leg and a shooting pain took my breath away. The woman in red patted my hand. "Gladys, wet me a towel. Cold water," she directed. Gladys hopped up and asked one of the gawking women to hold the pin.

When I came to the second time, the restroom had cleared and the music out in the club had stopped. It was so quiet you could've heard a pin drop. But not mine; the woman named Gladys was again sitting at my feet, smoking a cigarette with one hand and holding up the straight pin from my belt with the other.

"The cops came," the red satin lady said, mopping my brow with the damp paper towel. "You were lucky, sister."

What was she talking about? Had the cops come to help me? I didn't have a chance to find out because a woman burst in and pointed at me. "Her man's comin' in," she shouted.

Jim stepped in frowning, scooped me up and carried me out, down the creaky wooden stairs and several blocks to his car. He didn't say a word so I figured he was furious; turned out he was concerned about my knee, which had swollen to soccer ball size. As he settled me into the backseat, I groaned.

"Let's head for the ER," he said. "Grady's two minutes from here."

"No, I'm fine," I protested. "Just take me to Pam's."

"Uh . . . she won't be there. She and Andy got hauled off in a paddy wagon."

"Huh?"

"Cops raided the place."

"Oh, no! Poor Pam," I said, realizing what the woman had meant when she said I was lucky. If I hadn't been laid out moaning in the restroom, they would've nabbed me too. My young white face would've stood out like a searchlight on a dark night. "Why didn't they arrest you?" I asked Jim. "You're not twenty-one either."

"I don't know; I guess they didn't notice me."

Like I said before, he was short.

Jim stopped at an all-night gas station, got me a Coke, and delivered me home. He steadied me as I perched on one foot and quietly unlocked the door. No "thanks for everything" from me; I was focused on getting to my bed. After he drove off I hopped down the hall—the long, long hall—to my room, pausing three or four times to rest.

My shoes had disappeared in the confusion; my pin had not. As I struggled to get undressed, I discovered it in my belt. Apparently, one of those angels of mercy had hastily reinserted it before Jim hauled me away.

The next morning my parents bought my story about slipping while bowling, though they questioned why I'd worn my best dress to Buckhead Lanes. Dad took me to the hospital, where an x-ray revealed that my knee was dislocated—no broken bones. It was not pleasant when the doc "relocated" it and wrapped it in a mile-long Ace bandage, but at least I got to go home. My family pampered me for weeks as I hobbled around on crutches.

Pam didn't fare as well. She'd been thrown in the drunk tank with prostitutes and homeless women, and her mother wasn't thrilled about having to bail her out at six in the morning. Who knows what happened to Andy; we never heard from him—or Jim—again.

Pam and I live on different coasts now, but we stay in touch; once in a while we reminisce about our foolhardy teenage escapades, most notably the fiasco with the college boys. Recalling that night I still feel grateful to those kind women who safeguarded my pin, making sure I left the Royal Peacock Social Club as "put together" as I'd been when I arrived.

Confessions of a Clotheshorse

WHEN I WAS A teenager, a therapist might have dubbed me an addict. I would've disagreed; I simply loved clothes. Nothing delighted me more than trotting off to a cute boutique or department store. I'm stealing a line from *West Side Story*, but I now believe I was "depraved on account of being deprived."

My obsession started after years of wearing a boring private school uniform: gray pleated skirt, white blouse, dark navy blazer. My psyche was crying out for color, but we weren't allowed to snazz up that drab outfit. It was the early 1960s, and madras was the rage. But, no, we couldn't even add a madras hair band or belt; no flashy jewelry either. A bright red purse might get you expelled.

I begged my parents to let me go to public school with my neighborhood friends, and by my senior year they finally agreed. Set free from that stuffy institution, my inner clotheshorse went wild. A wide open range awaited me; Atlanta's first mall, Lenox Square, was five minutes from our house.

On Saturdays, my John Romaine pocketbook packed with Daddy's little metal Charga-Plates, I hit the stores. Soon my closet was crammed with short wool skirts and jumpers (we called them "knee-ticklers"), stacks of sweaters in jewel tones, oxford cloth blouses, boots and loafers—Weejuns, of course. My top dresser drawer overflowed with bangle bracelets, long gold chains, circle pins, and costume watches.

Salesladies at the small shops knew me by name. Their happy, high-pitched whinnies greeted me whenever I arrived. They must have been working on commission.

In June, after graduation, my father had to rein me in. I'd just pranced in with three new swimsuits: a royal blue one-piece with a flirty skirt; one of the new two-piece suits—cream piped in navy; and a Hawaiian print maillot.

"Honey," Daddy said, "I can't keep up with your spending." My father never, ever raised his voice, but on this day I could see that he was serious. His face was as chalk-white as the stack of bills he clutched in his hand. "You've got to stay out of the stores."

I complied. There was no way around it, as he had confiscated all the Charga-Plates in their sleek leather cases. But it wasn't too traumatic; I had amassed enough outfits to carry me through college.

I kept my binge shopping under control for years, then fell off the wagon after a second period of extreme deprivation. During my senior year in college I fell in love with Mr. Wrong and married him the day after my twenty-first birthday. This fellow did not understand basic needs like keeping up with the latest styles and buying clothes to lift one's spirits. He corralled his clotheshorse bride and tethered her to a tight budget.

We were both working full-time and could easily afford spiffy wardrobes, but I didn't protest. I hadn't taken assertiveness classes yet and went along with the miser. For five long years I subsisted on a diet of six dresses and two pairs of shoes. OK, I exaggerate . . . but not much.

To cheer me up after the divorce, two of my girlfriends suggested a trip. It was just what I needed: a two-week, thousand-mile journey up the Eastern Seaboard to sightsee—and shop. Between Atlanta and our final destination, we stayed with relatives or friends in six states; that translates into lots of shopping.

There was no such thing as an outlet mall in 1972, but individual outlets were plentiful in the cities we visited. I arrived home with hot pants, maxi skirts, minis, and midis. I hit the mother lode on coats: a London Fog trench, a plum-colored wool maxi with fur collar and cuffs, a wheat-colored all-weather midi with white faux fur at the collar and hem. Oh, and white leather boots to match. At a Vanity Fair warehouse sale, I loaded up on peignoirs in sherbet colors; I also bought bras, panties, and slips that matched; camisoles, socks, and hose.

Back in Atlanta I considered leasing a barn for my plunder; that didn't pan out, however, given the frightening balance on my credit card. I chipped away at that debt for several years. Husband #2 later confessed that he'd waited to propose till my balance was zero.

After marrying Mr. Right, I continued to keep my addiction in check. Buying and furnishing our first house became priorities. In fact, I was more interested in nesting than shopping for many years. Then it happened: in the early eighties consignment stores began to crop up, and the clotheshorse within me reemerged with a vengeance. To my mind, resale shopping was a fresh new pasture and I galloped in.

To this day I still graze in that fertile land, finding great "gently worn" clothing but never breaking the bank. And in the mountains where I live now, a turtleneck, jeans, and comfortable earth shoes are all I need.

Unhinged

JAN COULDN'T UNDERSTAND why her friends still wanted to "fix her up." She'd been divorced five years and never once complained about being single. Several of them had even suggested that she register with one of those awful online dating sites. Maybe they wanted her married so they could include her in their couples' parties. Apparently, setting a table for an odd number is a challenge.

On the one hand Jan thought it was sweet that they wanted her to be happy. On the other hand it rankled. Did they view her as half a person because she didn't have a husband? Sometimes she wanted to lash out, say something hurtful like "You don't always seem thrilled with married life." Two friends bitched about their husbands constantly, then—sometimes in the same conversation—bemoaned the fact that Jan was alone.

Yes, she thought, I am alone. But I'm not lonely. So when Shelley called to ask if she could give Jan's number to a neighbor, Owen somebody, she said thanks but no thanks.

Shelley sighed. "He just wants to meet for coffee."

"Well ... I don't know." She drew in a deep breath. "Does he read?"

"Of course he reads; he has a PhD."

"In what? Palm reading?"

"Very funny. No, anthropology."

"Oh, goodie. We can chat about the mating habits of primitive Samoans."

"For Pete's sake, Jan, give him a chance."

"You know, you've been married so long you don't understand this, but dating's awkward when you're closing in on Medicare."

"You're not even sixty!"

"Listen, I'm doing just fine. I'm proving what Gloria Steinem said—"

"What'd she say?"

"That you don't need a man to be happy. Besides, even if I did fall for some guy, he'd take one look at me and bolt."

"Jan? Owen Miller here. Shelley Wells' friend."

Hmm. Nice voice.

"Have you got a few minutes?"

"Sure."

"Shelley says we have a lot in common. I understand you're from Savannah too . . ."

Jan stretched out on the couch, talked to Owen for an hour. They didn't discuss their failed marriages and, yes, they did share similar interests: photography, classical music, old movies. She hung up thinking it might be a nice change to go out with a man now and then; she had plenty of women friends. And going out for coffee was no big deal. If they hit it off they could move on to lunch. If they didn't, she'd only lose an hour or two out of her day.

The next morning she called Shelley.

"Did he ask you out?"

"Yep, but I'm too busy right now."

"Jan!"

"Calm down. We're getting together on the fifteenth."

"Why are you putting this off? You're not going for a root canal."

"I need a haircut."

"Well, make an appointment today; if you wait too long you'll back out."

"I don't understand Jan," Shelley told her husband at breakfast. Hank was staring out the window, probably wondering if his golf game was still on, she imagined.

"Umm," he said, glancing over at her. "What's she up to?"

"I'm trying to get her to go out with Owen Miller, but she's making excuses."

"Seems like an okay guy."

"She needs to get out. She's a workaholic."

"Umm."

"She's lovely and smart and funny . . . other people move on after a divorce . . . I don't know, I guess her ex really did a number on her."

"She's been divorced how long?"

"Five years. She's only had two dates in five years!" Hank looked at his watch, then out the window again as Shelley got up and began clearing dishes. "She says she's a feminist, but she's so worried about how she looks. Thinks she's fat."

"Wonder if Owen plays golf . . ."

The day after agreeing to meet Owen, Jan started a 1200-calorie diet, walked three miles around Lake Pearson, and made an appointment with Tammy for a haircut. She assessed her wardrobe and decided that everything in her closet was drab or tired-looking, so she took off for the mall. She came home with three sweaters, a skirt, and two pairs of slacks. She didn't plan to keep them all, but in the cramped dressing room it was hard to tell which was most flattering.

Jan tried on the new pieces in various combinations. Nothing worked but the green sweater, which complemented her hazel eyes, but she looked dumpy in the skirt and the slacks were ho-hum. She sighed, left everything on the bed, and went back to her office.

After four hours at the computer she'd gotten nowhere, and she had only till Friday to produce three potential logos for a used car company to choose from. They wanted to improve their image. Jan doubted that any logo would help; they were a run-of-the-mill dealership with sleazy salesmen in ill-fitting suits. Still, she had to try; the money was good and winter was fast approaching. Over the years as a freelance graphic designer, her business had always slowed down in January.

Jan wondered if designers get "blocked" like writers. She never had, so she figured the impending date was distracting her. She turned off the computer and headed for the kitchen, poured a glass of merlot—something she rarely did—and sat down at the breakfast bar. What was her problem? She'd left Savannah after the divorce, struck out on her own to a small town in the North Carolina mountains, and made new friends. She loved her little cottage and the beauty of the area, and she claimed she wasn't interested in a relationship. So why was she suddenly behaving like a fifteen-year-old?

"I need a manicure but I can't afford it," Jan whined to Shelley over lunch. Shelley was diving into a plump chicken wrap while Jan pushed her tiny green salad, sans dressing, around the plate.

"Men don't notice fingernails, Jan! Aren't you always saying men should love us for what's inside?'"

"Well, they should. But if they hate our packaging they don't stick around to discover our souls."

She went on to tell Shelley about her shopping spree and her experiment with a drugstore hair color, which turned out orange and had to be corrected by Tammy to the tune of eighty-five dollars. She also mentioned her speed-walking regimen. "Owen told me he works out every day."

Shelley shook her head. "I don't think he's expecting you to be an Olympiad."

On the morning of the date Shelley phoned Jan. "I'm no psychic, but I've got a good feeling about this," she chirped. "What time are you meeting?"

"Three o'clock, I hope."

"Whaddaya mean, 'you hope'?"

"My stomach's upset."

"It's just butterflies." Shelley giggled. She sounded giddy, Jan thought, like she was the one with the date. "What're you wearing?"

"The new sweater. Oh, and Sergio gave me a great cut."

"Who? I thought Tammy cut it."

"Yeah, but it was uneven."

"Who's Sergio?"

"I thought I told you. A woman in line at the post office had a fantastic hairstyle and . . . anyway, long story. She gave me his number."

Jan arrived at the café and waited at a table out front. She loved Picasso's and usually enjoyed their lattes, but today she was a wreck. She adjusted her turtleneck, squinted at her reflection in the café window and patted her hair down at the crown. After noticing her thighs spread out across the little bistro chair, she decided to stand up. She scanned the sidewalk in both directions. Nothing. Just a teenager checking his cell phone and a gangly old man limping along behind him. As they passed, the old guy veered off and approached her. "Jan?" he said, sun glinting off his wire-rim glasses.

She narrowed her eyes. "Yes?"

"Owen Miller." He didn't smile but reached out to shake her hand.

"Oh! I'm sorry I didn't recognize you. You look . . . uh . . . different from the picture you e-mailed."

He looked away, sort of shifty-like, muttered that it was "taken a while back."

So, she thought, men angst over their looks too.

They sat down and right away Owen frowned and turned up the collar on his windbreaker, shivering.

"Want to move inside?" Jan asked in her sweetest Southern belle voice, the one that still popped out around men now and then. The message it conveyed was, "Honey, I'll do anything your little ol' heart desires to make you happy." She wanted to slap herself.

"No," he grumbled, hunching down in his chair. He looked so

miserable, she figured he'd sized her up and wasn't impressed. Well, so what? She wasn't exactly bowled over; nevertheless, she soldiered on with small talk.

"Did you go to the gym today?"

He didn't answer, just pulled a notepad out of his pocket. "OK, let's get to it."

"Get to what?"

"Are you interested in a committed relationship?"

"Excuse me?"

"Are you willing to winter in Florida?"

"I didn't get to answer your—"

"You don't have pets, I hope; I'm highly allergic."

On and on, he fired questions; occasionally Jan was able to squeeze in a reply. No chit-chat. No getting-to-know-you conversation. Only the business at hand—interviewing her for the hausfrau position.

In one hour she was back in her home office, a hint of soured latte lingering in her mouth. She mulled over how much to tell Shelley, who loved playing matchmaker. Since this fix-up had crashed and burned like the *Hindenburg*, Jan decided to leave out the details; no need to rub it in. Of course, that meant she couldn't brag about getting bolder as Owen's cross-examination progressed. Or that she got downright cheeky when he asked if she could cook. "I microwave a mean Lean Cuisine," she'd said.

Jan's phone rang nonstop after dinner. First caller: Shelley. She gasped after hearing only the abbreviated version of the meeting.

"So he just dismissed you?"

"Yep. I didn't even make the short list."

"Oh, Jan, I had no idea he was such a jerk."

"No worries. When we talked on the phone, he fooled me too."

Next her old friend Carole called from Savannah. Then Megan, Jan's daughter, who sounded as disappointed as Shelley. Even Jan's neighbor asked over the fence how her "hot date" went. "Oh, fine," she said, unwilling to discuss it again. "Interesting guy. We just didn't click." Walking away, she shuddered at the ease with which she'd lied. And why?

She supposed it was easier to tell people what she assumed they wanted to hear. Being raised in the South before women's lib had ruined her, programmed her to always be pleasant, never discuss problems. As a result of following those rules, she rarely knew how she felt about anything. And after catering to Kip for so many years, she didn't even know what she wanted for dinner most of the time, much less what she wanted her future to look like. But tonight, she was sure about one thing: she would tell no one she'd spent close to three hundred dollars preparing for thirty minutes with a grouchy geezer. On the upside, though, she was pleased with her new hairstyle and the green sweater; plus, she was excited about eating real meals again. She'd been so hungry for two weeks she could've eaten Kleenex.

Jan completed the logo for the used car people on time. They raved, said she'd "hit the nail on the head," and hired her to design several direct mail pieces for them. But as she'd anticipated, her workload dwindled after Christmas. Now she had time to bundle up, hike on trails off the Blue Ridge Parkway several times a week. On one of those outings she tried to analyze why one blind date had unhinged her. Why had she thought she needed a complete overhaul, like a beat-up old car? After all, Kip hadn't traded her in for a new model. He'd divorced her to marry his frumpy-dumpy secretary, not a gorgeous younger woman.

So what was her problem? She tried to be stylish and look her best, but she had never obsessed about it. She'd always thought it was shallow for women to fixate on their looks. How, how, how could she be almost sixty years old and know so little about herself? And really, she wondered, how much longer did she have to get acquainted with the real Jan?

Luck

JOANNA'S HANDS TREMBLED as she backed out of her parking space at the college. She knew it was irrational, but just having her student's gift in the car made her uneasy. Abbie had presented it to her as they left for Christmas break, said she'd worked on it for several months. Although it was beautiful, Joanna couldn't wait to get rid of it.

"Do you know about dream catchers?" Abbie had asked.

"Not really."

"I sort of figured you wouldn't, so . . . here, I pulled this off the Web for you."

Abbie handed her a small square of parchment paper. On it she had printed: *The dream catcher is round like the circle of life. The web catches your good dreams but lets the bad ones pass through the hole in the center.*

"How lovely," Joanna said.

"You hang it over your bed for good luck. My grandma swore these things work. She was Cheyenne River Sioux."

Joanna drove about a mile from the college, turned into a McDonald's and pulled around to the back. She studied the dream catcher—the rich brown leather, the bead work, the delicate golden feathers. Abbie had obviously spent many hours crafting the piece. But there was no way she could keep it, not after what happened last year with the so-called "lucky buckeye."

Joanna scanned the parking lot. No one was around, so she parked and got out with the dream catcher in hand. She was ready to toss it in the dumpster, but when she saw the wilted lettuce, the ketchup-laden half-eaten buns, the greasy smashed cardboard boxes—all crawling with flies—she couldn't bring herself to throw someone's work of art into this slop. Maybe her friend Nan would like it.

"Of course I'll take it," Nan said. "I'll hang it on the wall right now. Here, over my computer. Maybe it'll catch my dream to write a best seller."

"I wouldn't bet on it," Joanna said.

Nan asked why she was so edgy and Joanna told her about the buckeye incident last fall.

Joanna's paintings had suddenly stopped selling, which had pounded her ego and rendered her unable to paint. She'd heard about "blocked" artists and thought it was a bunch of hooey. But after several weeks of staring at a blank canvas, she realized she was indeed blocked. Then one day her quirky next-door neighbor presented her with a buckeye, which looked like a chestnut to Joanna. "Tuck it in your pocket and carry it at all times," Margie had advised. "It'll bring you good luck."

"Yippee," Joanna said. "I need some luck, and I need it now."

Several days later, she found a thick padded mailer wedged in her mailbox. The gallery in Atlanta that had been reviewing slides of her work—for months—had returned them with a form rejection letter. Thanks, but no thanks.

It was a sparkling fall day and Joanna had driven home from class with her sunroof open, singing along with the radio. She'd stopped for a take-out gyro at her favorite Greek restaurant. Now she wasn't hungry and plopped the sandwich in the fridge.

Tell yourself the same thing you tell your students when they get rejections, she thought. Shake it off and send your work back out right away.

Joanna flipped through the rest of her mail, pondering where to send the slides next, then ripped open an envelope from the company that managed the condominium complex she lived in. All twenty-nine units needed new roofs and the owners were being assessed several thousand dollars.

Since Joanna had a mortgage and second mortgage on her condo, and two credit cards nearly maxed out, this was not good news. Her mind raced through its usual paces. What could she sell? Grandma's crystal? No, most of it was chipped. The handmade bed Aunt Corinne left her? But then where would she sleep? This line of thinking generally led to imagining herself homeless, but she was interrupted by the phone ringing.

"Joanna? June Ernst. I hate to cancel at this late date, but Sam can't come for his art lesson on Saturday. We've got family business in Charlotte and need to take him with us. I'm so sorry."

Joanna muttered something in response, though when she hung up she wasn't sure what it had been. She rummaged through the pile of letters and folders on her desk until she uncovered a file marked "Bills." Which one would she not be able to pay because Sam Ernst wouldn't be taking his lesson?

At this point she had developed a growling headache and decided to stretch out for a nap, something she only did when her life was teetering out of control. As she hung up her slacks, the buckeye fell out of the pocket. She scooped it up, deposited it in her jewelry box, and slammed it shut.

"Hey, Mom, how's it going?"

Joanna didn't recall picking up the phone. At first, she wasn't sure it was Lauren, thought she might be dreaming. "Honey, is that you?"

"What's wrong? You sound weird."

"Oh, bad day . . . I was asleep. What's up?"

"Well, I hate to make your day worse, but Dad bailed out on paying for my textbooks."

"Why? What did he say, Lauren?"

"He just said he can't do it right now. My books cost three hundred dollars, and I need them Monday."

"Damn him! That man never, ever . . ." Joanna stopped herself. She'd vowed long ago not to bad-mouth her ex in front of her daughter. Lauren had been hurt enough. "Honey, I just don't have it."

"I know, Mom. But I was thinking about that old Russian stamp collection. The one Dad gave me. Could we sell it?"

"I have no idea where it is."

"It's in my closet. Up on the top shelf."

Joanna found the album, made some calls, and connected with the head of a local philatelists' club. The man happened to specialize in Russian stamps and wanted to see them right away. The next morning he was sitting at her kitchen table paging through the thick album, a hungry look in his eyes. Joanna sensed that he wanted the collection, or part of it, which would be wonderful. Instant cash!

"Could I take this home with me for a day or two?" he asked after scanning only a few pages. "To give you an accurate figure, I need to check my catalogs."

Several of Joanna's friends knew this man; she felt sure he wouldn't skip town with the album, so she agreed. She tried to appear blasé about the whole thing. If he wanted the stamps and she seemed desperate, he might lowball her on his offer.

After he pulled out of her driveway, she retrieved the buckeye from her jewelry box, where she'd slung it into a snarl of bracelets and hoop earrings. She went into the den and Googled "buckeye for luck" on her laptop. Multiple sites popped up and she opened the first one. It confirmed what her neighbor had said, that nuts from buckeye trees were considered good luck. Someone on the next site, a blog, claimed buckeyes could heal arthritis and rheumatism if you placed them under your mattress.

"Ridiculous," Joanna said out loud, then headed for the kitchen. While her low carb "California spa" meal was heating, she studied the buckeye. Other than its little cream-colored eye, it looked like a rather ordinary brown nut to her. Nevertheless, she began rubbing it with her thumb, then polished it with a dish towel.

She watched her lunch rotating in the microwave and fretted over Lauren's dilemma. She was on a full scholarship at Appalachian State, but Kent had promised to help her with textbooks and activity fees.

This was so typical of him—to not only let her down, but to do it at the last minute. Joanna had scrounged enough money to buy Lauren a clunker car to get around campus, and she'd charged the student health policy on her credit card. But now facing mounting bills, she could do no more.

That evening Joanna watched the news, then switched over to a rerun of *What Not To Wear.* She wished someone would nominate her for that show. She'd get her free makeover and five thousand dollars' worth of clothes, then dash back to Asheville and sell them. Even a thousand would cover Lauren's books for the year.

By ten o'clock the dull headache she'd waked up with had escalated to near-migraine level, so she took three ibuprofen and crawled into bed with a chilled gel-pack for her throbbing eyes. She slept fitfully at first, then descended into a heavy, dreamless sleep. Bright sun rays were streaming in through the blinds when the phone woke her. It was Mr. Fischer, the stamp collector.

Joanna knew from his tone that the news wasn't good. Apparently, important stamps were missing from more than a dozen pages. "It doesn't appear to be a random thing," he said. "It's not as if a few fell out . . . or were never acquired . . . they've been carefully removed."

Had Kent pillaged the most valuable stamps? If so, how could he do that to Lauren?

"What do you think the album's worth, Mr. Fischer?"

"I doubt you'd get more than a few hundred dollars, if that." Joanna was silent. "I'm sorry," he said. "I'll bring it back tomorrow."

She padded out to the kitchen, brewed coffee, and stared out the window. The leaves had been falling for weeks and she could now see the Singletons' house deep in the woods. Neighbors said they were a wealthy Florida couple who had built the enormous gabled house as a summer home. But in the three years Joanna had lived in her condo, she'd seen cars there only once or twice.

I need a long walk, she thought, as she sipped her black coffee. She had to figure out what to do about Lauren. She wheeled away from the sink and headed for the bedroom; she yanked on jeans and a sweatshirt and grabbed the buckeye as she charged out the back door.

If a hiker had happened upon Joanna standing ankle-deep in the creek behind the Singletons' mansion, a crazed look in her eye, he would likely have called nine one one. Or at least wondered about the small round object she pulled from her pocket and threw so violently downstream.

Less than twenty-four hours after she'd disposed of the buckeye, she received two calls, one after the other. The first was from the manager of the Blue Spiral Gallery, one of Asheville's best; she wondered if Joanna would be interested in a one-woman show. The second was Lauren; her father had e-mailed to say he was sending the money for her books. "He said he had a windfall, Mom, whatever that means."

As Joanna shared the news about the gallery with Lauren, she heard sirens—close by. "Gotta run," she said, and from her window she watched in horror as angry flames licked the sky above the Singletons' home, black smoke billowing.

Now sitting in Nan's office, Joanna admitted she'd had nightmares for weeks after that. "I guess I felt sort of responsible."

Nan shook her head. "Get a grip," she said, stepping back to admire the dream catcher she had hung while Joanna unraveled her tale. "Surely you don't think a little nut caused that fire."

Reunion

THE PULLEYS SQUEAKED as they lowered my mother's casket into the grave, freshly dug in our family plot at Atlanta's historic Oakland Cemetery. Not another sound, just the squeaking. No rustle of leaves in the stately old oaks. Not one sniffle or sigh. Genteel southerners, white Protestant southerners, don't wail and beat their breasts at funerals. But as the first shovelful of dirt was tossed in the hole, a moan came from the road. Then, "Oh, Miz Claiborne. Oh, sweet Jesus," followed by sobbing.

My father didn't notice, but my aunts looked astonished when I rose from the metal folding chair and threaded myself through the cluster of friends and relatives. Out by the hearse was a short, round black woman in a gray uniform and white apron; the apron, I could see as I approached her, was covered with dark red stains, stains the color of blood. And when I got closer, I saw that it was Etha Mae.

"Lawd, have mercy, Miss Sarah," she wailed, fumbling and dropping her big straw pocketbook on the grass.

I grabbed her and held her. "How did you know, Mae? How did you get here?"

"Oh, sweet Jesus, your poor mama."

I pulled away from her and looked down into her broad, dark face. "Why would you come here, Mae? How could you forgive her? How could you possibly forgive her?"

I hadn't seen Etha Mae Sellars since my sophomore year in college. I'd come home for spring break and she was gone, "let go," my mother said, because she'd gotten lazy. But Mae's problems with Mother had started long before that—back in 1961, the year Mother turned to scotch to help her through the day. She'd had cancer and was terrified it would come back, even though they'd removed her breast, told her they were sure they'd gotten it all. Etha Mae kept all of us fed, made sure my father's shirts were starched and ironed, and that our home was immaculate. This went on for a year, and when we moved to a larger house—Daddy's attempt to cheer up Mother—Mae continued to keep things running smoothly.

When I got home from school every day, our house was dark and quiet as death. Mother insisted on keeping the shutters closed and drapes drawn, even when she was holed up in her bedroom nursing a hangover. Mae was always downstairs in the laundry room, so I would grab a Coke and go down to chat with her.

I spent countless hours perched on a tall wooden stool in our cellar watching Mae iron. When we weren't talking, she would sing in her rich alto voice, usually a Negro spiritual or a hymn she'd learned at church. She would start out humming, then break into a song about how much she loved Jesus. "Sometimes I get so full of the Holy Spirit, I almost bust," she would say, laughing and crying at the same time. But then she'd blow her nose, straighten her apron, and go right back to ironing.

Mother hated my spending so much time with Mae. She'd concoct a reason to get me back upstairs as soon as she discovered where I was.

"When we fraternize with hired help, they forget they're employees and the quality of their work plummets," she lectured. "Now, we are all deeply devoted to Etha Mae, but you must not fraternize with her."

"What's 'fraternize'?" I asked, smart-alecky.

"Don't get petulant with me, Sarah. Someday you'll be married and have your own home, and you'll thank me for this instruction. Servants know their place, and they want *us* to remember ours. It makes them terribly uncomfortable when we don't."

I ignored her and visited with Etha Mae whenever I felt like it. I don't think Mother believed a word of her fraternizing speech. On many occasions I saw her eating lunch in the kitchen with Mae, talking with her like a friend. I think she was just jealous because, like a typical teenager, I'd stopped sharing my personal life with her.

The laundry room at our house smelled like a mixture of Georgia red clay, soap, and starch. A strange odor, but to me it smelled *real*—alive. Upstairs there was no odor at all. It was as if our house had been sealed like a tomb, with thick gray air trapped in it. The air at my school, the Howell School, was stale and gray too, to match our uniforms. After enduring that oppressive atmosphere all day, it was a relief to sit in the cellar with Etha Mae. Hearing her humming, her iron hissing on the damp clothes, gave me the same relaxed feeling I get when a hairdresser shampoos my hair, massages my head and neck.

I still recall a conversation Mae and I once had down there. "How you likin' school this year, Miss Sarah?" she asked me.

"Hate it," I said, making a gagging sound in my throat. "The girls giggle all the time and the boys are all weird. Look, here's how they wear their pants." I hiked my skirt up to my chest and walked with my pelvis stuck out.

Mae threw her head back and howled, gold fillings flashing.

"Etha Mae!" my mother bellowed from the top of the stairs.

"Yessum, Miz Claiborne?"

"Is Sarah down there?"

"Yes, ma'am."

"Well, send her upstairs, please."

Up I went. "What?"

She motioned me into the kitchen. "Don't 'what' me, Sarah. I'm sure you have homework and I want you to do it. Your father is paying a fortune for Howell, and he expects you to apply yourself."

Suddenly it hit me: I had grown over the summer and was now looking directly at her, not cowering as she glared down at me. "I'll come up in a little while," I said, then turned and casually proceeded down the hall and back down the steps.

"Sarah, come here this instant. You will not put off your homework until you're too tired to think!" Her voice rumbled down the stairwell after me, words ricocheting off the bare walls.

I kept going.

That act of insubordination was the beginning of Mae's troubles. Mother rode her unmercifully, criticized everything she did. She'd left the pickle relish out of the egg salad. She'd ironed my father's shirt collars the wrong way. Pick, pick, pick. Then, in the fall of my senior year, she accused her of stealing silverware, fired her, and sent her home with no severance pay.

I was devastated; I'd known Mae all my life! Mother smirked when she saw me sulking. Her expression said, "You have no one to blame but yourself."

I did feel it was my fault. I wanted to see Mae, apologize, find out if she was okay. But there was no way. I had no address for her, and if she and her husband, Troop, had a phone it wasn't listed. I had a general idea of where her neighborhood was; I'd ridden out there with my parents a half dozen times. It was way out, off the Bankhead Highway. Twice after school I tried to find it, drove up and down, street after street, but never spotted their little brick house with the rose bush out front.

A month later, Etha Mae was back, rehired by Mother for selfish reasons, of course. My brother was playing baseball and coming home from practices and games with his socks and uniforms caked in red mud—almost impossible to wash out according to detergent commercials on TV.

All was well for Mae after that—Mother needed her—until I came home from college to find that she'd been fired again, this time for good. Following in my footsteps, my younger sister had taken to "fraternizing" with her too often. And that was that. Once again, I wanted to find her. My father gave me the last address he had for her—to send her a reference, which Mother refused to do—but she and Troop had moved, left no forwarding address. When she showed up at Mother's funeral, I hadn't seen her for seven years.

At the cemetery, I calmed Etha Mae enough to learn that she'd seen Mother's obituary in the paper. She was working in the kitchen at Peachtree Golf Club and was so shaken she left the rare roast beef she was carving and took two buses to get there.

People began walking out to their cars; the service had ended.

"What happened to your mama?" Mae asked, mopping her face with a big white handkerchief.

"Heart attack in her armchair . . . watching Johnny Carson," I told her. "Guess all the drinking . . ." I shrugged, but then my throat closed and I teared up.

Mae put her hand on my arm. "I missed y'all, Miss Sarah," she said. "I prayed for you. I put Miz Claiborne on the prayer list at Ebenezer."

"Why, Mae? Why didn't you hate her? She was awful to you."

"Lawd, chile, I loved yo mama! She was hurtin'. After she come back from the hospital that time—after that cancer—she never did get right. Never got her ol' self back. No, honey, I couldn't hate her. I saw she was hurtin' real bad."

Mae must have seen on my face that I didn't understand, but she just smiled and patted my arm.

"Oh, Mae, I'm married and we've got a little girl."

"Lawd have mercy, Miss Sarah, you all grown up!"

"Will you call me? Will you come see us . . . see my baby?"

"I will, Miss Sarah. You know I will!"

She kept her promise and we stayed in touch until she died—only four years after we found each other. I still think of her often, especially on Mother's Day. At first I think about my mother, how miserable the last years of her life were, how depressed she was. But then I remember Mae, and some little girl part of me wishes I could just curl up for a while in her soft lap and listen to her sing.

Acknowledgments

Many thanks to the editors of the journals and anthologies in which the following stories first appeared, some in slightly different form:

"Stung" in *Pisgah Review*
"The Bridge" in *Emrys Journal*
"Watching for Signs" (under the title "Manna from Heaven") in *Moonshine Review*
"Choked Up" in *Pisgah Review*
"Shame on Me" in *Moonshine Review*
"The Decision" (under the title "A Road as Wide as the World") in *Wild Violet*
"Memory of Fire" in *The Sun* (Readers' Write)
"S.O.S." in *Long Story Short*
"Reunion" in *Moonshine Review*
"Watching for Signs" appeared in the anthology *Echoes Across the Blue Ridge: Stories, Essays, and Poems*, Ed.: Nancy Simpson, Winding Path Publishing, 2010.
"Confessions of a Clotheshorse" appeared in the anthology *Clothes Lines*, Eds.: Celia H. Miles and Nancy Dillingham, Catawba Publishing, 2009.

For their careful reading and critique of the "almost" final draft of *A Closet Full of Masks*, the novella in this collection, I am most grateful to writers Marian Gowan and Lana Hendershott; their feedback was invaluable.

I also appreciate two authors whose books gave me insight into the Bible Belt ethos. They are Susan Ketchin, author of *The Christ-Haunted Landscape: Faith and Doubt in Southern Fiction* (University Press of Mississippi, 1994), *and Tanya Luhrmann, author of When God Talks Back: Understanding the American Evangelical Relationship with God* (Knopf Doubleday Publishing Group, 2012).

Praise for Susan Snowden's Novel *Southern Fried Lies*

2013 Independent Publisher Gold Medal for Fiction in the Southeast

"*Southern Fried Lies* is a riveting read about family and the period (1960s) . . . Highly recommended."

– *Midwest Book Review* (Reviewer's Choice)

"Southern Fried Lies delivers . . . thoroughly engaging . . . a driving plot . . . a narrator we come to love."

– Rob Neufeld, *Asheville Citizen-Times*

"What a tough, touching, humorous, often unsettling novel Susan Snowden has written."

– Anthony Bukoski, author of *Time Between Trains*

"It's been a long time since I've come across a book so flawlessly written and a story so compellingly told. One of those novels where words melt from the page and you forget you are reading."

– Lonnie Busch, author of *Turnback Creek*

"'People everywhere lie, not just in the South, and always for the same reason—to be loved,' writes Susan Snowden in her profoundly felt novel. This is not only a powerful family study, it's a keep-you-up-late page-turner. I highly recommend this debut book."

– Judy Goldman, author of *Losing My Sister*

"Transcends time . . . speaks to women of all ages . . . characters breathe and live as we do . . . Snowden captivates us with her details."

– Anne Hicks, *Main Street Rag*

"Though the title indicates a spoof on southern life, discerning readers realize by the prologue's end that Sarah Claiborne's story will not be frivolous . . . (yet) Sarah's dry humor often lends her perspectives a delightfully outrageous twist."

– Mary Ickes, *Western North Carolina Woman*

CPSIA information can be obtained
at www.ICGtesting.com
Printed in the USA
FFOW01n1705190915
17036FF

9 780985 330170